Cassandra Parkin has a Master's degree in English Literature from York University and has been writing fiction all her life—mostly as Christmas and birthday presents for friends and family. She is married with two children, has so far resisted her clear destiny to become a mad old cat lady, and lives in a small but perfectly-formed village in East Yorkshire. *New World Fairy Tales* is her first published book and winner of the Scott Prize.

CASSANDRA PARKIN

New World Fairy Tales

SALT

LONDON

PUBLISHED BY SALT PUBLISHING
Acre House, 11-15 William Road, London NW1 3ER United Kingdom

© Cassandra Parkin, 2011

The right of Cassandra Parkin to be identified as the author of this
work has been asserted by her in accordance with Section 77
of the Copyright, Designs and Patents Act 1988.

Printed in Great Britain by the MPG Books Group, Bodmin and King's Lynn

Typeset in Bembo 12 / 13.5

ISBN 978 1 8447 18 8 1 8 paperback

1 3 5 7 9 8 6 4 2

For Kim, Kate, Melissa, Heidi and AJ,
Who gave me inspiration
But most of all for Tony
Who gave me time, love and faith

Contents

Interview #4

—Ella Orlando
New Orleans, Louisiana

So, MY STORY? Well, it's your project, of course, but I don't think there's much to tell. Married twice, widowed once, two daughters by marriage. I've never liked the word 'stepchild'; it's a hard, ugly word. And no, I've never called myself a *stepmother* either.

Yes, that's the photo—rather worn and crumpled. He carried it all round town, you see, trying to find me, while I ran home to hide. The wildness of youth, although at the time I thought I was so *old* . . .

My dear, I do apologise. When we're young, we run; when we're old, we ramble. Well, let's start at the beginning—with the *first* time I got married.

Abbeville, 1964. Harry and I, drinking coffee in a diner, watching the rain. A long-haired couple, barefoot, even though it was pouring, stood at the bus stop kissing. When I looked at Harry, he was watching me watching them.

'I've never kissed you like that,' he said.

'You have,' I reminded him.

'But not in public.'

'So?'

He sighed.

'Oh, Ella, do I seem too old to you?'

'No,' I said and took his hand. The rain kissed the window. He was thirty-six years older than me.

'I'm plenty old enough to be your father.'

'That doesn't matter.'

'I've been married twice before.'

'I knew that when we met.'

'And I've got the girls . . .'

His daughters, Cindy and Beth. He hadn't married their mother.

'Why would that matter?'

'It's not much to offer, is it?' he tried to laugh. 'But for what it's worth, Ella—for what I'm worth—I'm all yours.'

'I know,' I said. Hot nights and stolen afternoons; motels and friend's houses and the back seat of his car. It meant something different back then. I was risking a lot—afraid he'd never call again, afraid I'd get caught—but I wanted to make him happy.

'I mean,' he said, 'I'll marry you, if you want to.' He kissed my hand. 'Would you like to? What do you think?'

I hadn't expected that. Sex simply wasn't something you did with a friend of your father, married twice before, whose last dalliance walked out on him to go and *find herself* in California. Not if you wanted a ring on your finger afterwards, anyway.

'Yes,' I said.

Oh, I know I've made him sound vile, but truly, he *wasn't*. He was loving, vulnerable, funny and clever, wise and charming and strong. I really don't think he knew, that day he proposed, that he was ill.

We had eight months before it got really bad—the pain breaking through the morphine, sheets soaked through with sweat. Even after the company folded—we'd had to leave the area after the wedding, it never ran right without him there—we were happy.

I nursed him myself, of course I did.

'You're sure you can do this?' he'd ask, nights when we'd sat up waiting for the dawn, and the nurse and the next morphine shot.

I held his hand.

'Yes,' I said.

Then he was gone and I had a failed business, a pile of bills, and two girls.

Our girls.

My girls, now. Pale faces and solemn eyes.

I vowed in the churchyard I'd make it up to them. I'd do everything for them, make them the centre of my world.

'If you need to come home . . .' My mother, caught between love and satisfaction at being proved right. She drew hard on her cigarette. 'But not his children. They can go to his sister's.'

'I'm staying with them,' I said.

'You're mad,' she told me. 'You don't have to.'

Their faces, so expectant and trusting. My heart turned over.

'Yes, I do,' I said. 'Don't make me choose, Mom, because I *will* choose them. I mean it.'

'You're serious?' She blew out smoke, looked at me in disbelief. 'You actually think you can raise those girls by yourself?'

'Yes,' I said.

1972: breakfast in a small house in Delacroix. Cindy was eleven, Beth was nine.

Cindy: 'I want a new dress for Linda's party.'

And Beth: 'I want one too. Can we have new dresses, Mom?'

The heel that came off my shoe that morning; that course I'd seen advertised, *Learn to type in six weeks*; the electricity bill. Their faces: expectant, confident. I swallowed.

'Yes,' I said.

'Cool,' said Cindy. 'Hey, you gave me the wrong cup!'

Cindy liked pink: pink bowl, pink cup, pink plate. Beth liked yellow. Cindy had wanted milk in bed last night, so the pink cup was dirty.

I went to the sink, found the pink cup, washed it. Cindy decanted her juice. It spilled everywhere. Cindy looked at it blankly.

I found a cloth, wiped the table, got onto the floor and wiped the floor.

From somewhere above me, Cindy said, 'I need more juice.'

I climbed out, got the juice, poured it, sat down again.

Beth said, 'I don't like cornflakes. I want Cap'n Crunch instead.'

I got up, poured Beth's cornflakes away, washed the bowl. Found the Cap'n Crunch. Filled the bowl, poured the milk.

Cindy said, 'There's the bus.'

Beth: 'I'll have a pop-tart instead.'

Cindy: 'I want a pop-tart too.'

I found the pop-tarts, gave them one each.

Beth said, 'We'll get the dresses after school, right?'

'Yes,' I said.

How can I explain —? Yes, they were selfish, but I wanted them to be. Their selfishness — their trust really, knowing I'd provide — showed I'd done my job, d'you see? A mom is supposed to be invisible. Or that's what I thought then, anyway.

Of course, there were times . . .

Delacroix, still; a different small house; 1978. Cindy was seventeen, Beth fifteen. I'd begun to wonder if life wasn't over for me, after all. Cindy's math teacher asked me to see *Star Wars*.

'I hope you're not shocked that teachers date,' he said. A nice, self-deprecating smile. I was thirty-two, but I didn't feel it.

'Yes,' I said. Surprising myself.

Cindy that afternoon: 'Mom, I need a lift to the bowling alley tonight. I'm meeting Andy.'

Beth said, 'If Cindy's going out, I am too.'

Cindy: 'You're not coming out with us! Tell her, Mom!'

Beth: 'I don't *want* to, it's *gross* watching you two make out. Mom, we'll go for pizza, okay? You'll like that.'

Cindy, anxious: 'But she needs to drop me off . . . wait, how about this. Mom drops me first, then takes you for pizza. Deal?'

Alex's serious brown eyes and tentative smile. It cost him a lot to ask. He'd never do it twice.

'Okay,' said Beth. 'Good idea. Isn't it, Mom?'

'Yes,' I said.

1983: Abbeville, again. My mom was dying. We hadn't spoken much, I hadn't been home at all, but some ties can't be broken.

'You'll come, won't you?' my dad asked. 'She wants to die at home . . .'

'Yes,' I said.

Two months it took. Cindy and Beth hated it. Who

could blame them? A small town, a dying grandmother, a distracted mother. No-one befriended them; it seemed disrespectful to the woman who lay gasping and choking, chained to the oxygen bottle, in the back room.

That last afternoon; my mother pressing an envelope into my hands.

'This is — for you,' she wheezed. 'Don't — open it — now. Wait until — you're alone — and I'm gone.' She stroked my hair. 'I love you — always did — it was *them* — I couldn't stand — they take advantage — of you — you're so sweet — my lovely — lovely Ella — love you so much . . .'

'I love you too,' I said.

'Do you — forgive me — for not — letting you — and his children — come home?'

'They're *mine*,' I said. 'I raised them. I love them. Please be nice, Mom, they're *my girls*.'

'You're too — too good — for this world,' she whispered.

I wiped away my tears and hers, and kissed her.

'Promise me.' She crumpled the envelope. 'Only — open it — when you're — when you're alone.'

'Yes,' I said.

Easy to say, but you try being alone with two curious young girls in the house.

No, I suppose they weren't really *girls* by then. Why, I was married at their age, married and widowed and responsible for them. And I'm damned glad their lives were different. I wanted more for them than I'd had. All parents do.

The envelope? Cindy opened it; she found it in my jewellery box. It was a cheque for a thousand dollars.

❧

'Grandma would have wanted us to enjoy this,' said Cindy, sitting at the table. 'I mean, it's a nice amount, but not life-changing, you know? Let's spend it on something fun.'

'Sounds good,' said Beth. She rested her beautiful face in her hands. 'Hey, how about New Orleans for Mardi Gras!'

'Oh, yes!' cried Cindy. 'A boarding house—we don't want a big hotel—meals out, and costumes . . .'

Open it on your own. I'm sorry, Mom. But you know how much you loved me? That's how much I love them. They can have anything, anything. The shirt off my back; the food from my mouth; the blood from my veins; the heart out of my body. A thousand dollars? That's nothing. Besides—New Orleans at Mardi Gras . . .

'Yes,' I said.

Two bedrooms and a bathroom in the French Quarter; faded furnishings, damp walls, high ceilings. Cindy said it smelled funny. Beth complained about the bathroom. I loved it.

'We'll buy costumes today,' said Cindy, in charge as usual. 'Fat Monday, Fat Tuesday, and the Krewe Balls.'

'If we're invited to them,' said Beth.

Cindy glanced at the old, spotted mirror. Long legs, blonde hair, an all-American smile. She smiled at Beth, small and sleek, with her father's glossy black hair and black eyes.

'We'll be invited,' she said. 'Won't we, Mom?'

'Yes,' I said.

A costumier's in the French Quarter. Beth and Cindy

romped through the shop as if they were six years old. Beth became a pirate, leather leggings and a striped jersey that turned her into a nineteen-sixties French model. Cindy chose a powder-blue dress with flirty wings and a flowered head-dress. Then a witch's dress for Beth, a columbine for Cindy. Finally, the costumier pulled back a curtain . . .

Ball gowns. Crimson and gold, scarlet, silver, violet, cerulean, apple; silk and satin and sequins. These were more like theatre than dressing-up; they were exquisite works of art; your heart beat faster just looking at them.

'A little more expensive,' purred the costumier. 'For hire only—with a deposit.'

Beth and Cindy were already choosing. I added up figures in my head, made a hard decision.

'Yes,' I said.

The girls chattered and laughed, making themselves beautiful. I told myself that was enough, they'd have fun without me, and what did I want with Mardi Gras, anyway? They didn't notice until they were leaving.

'I'm not coming,' I said. 'The ball gowns . . .' They looked guilty. 'It's all right. I don't mind. You have fun. Really.'

'I expect you'd rather not go out and party so soon after Grandma died,' said Cindy.

'We'll see you later,' said Beth, kissing me.

At the door, they saw my expression, and hesitated.

'Oh . . .' said Cindy.

'Is it really all right?' asked Beth.

'Yes,' I said.

And then they were gone.

I folded up discarded clothes. I put lids back on tubes and

tubs of cosmetics. I cleaned the bath. I made the beds. I threw out the trash. I wiped away tears.

After a while, someone thumped on the floor above me. A steady, regular whacking, made with a stick.

Hastily, I stopped crying. But the whacking went on. I sat mouse-still; someone who had a stick all ready might be hyper-sensitive to noise. The whacking went on. On and on and on.

Finally, I crept upstairs.

'Hello,' I said to the closed door.

'At last,' said a voice inside.

I opened the door and found an old lady lying on the floor and clutching a walking stick. She glared at me.

'You took your god-damn time,' she accused. 'What the hell kept you?'

I could see she was embarrassed, so I let her be cross. I helped her up, and into the bathroom; afterwards I helped her up again, and back to bed. She should really have had a nurse. Her hands were knotted tree roots, hot and swollen. She looked at me with bird-bright eyes.

'I'm Hazel,' she said. 'And you've done this before. Tell me who?'

She was imperious, and I was lonely.

'My husband. Then my mother.'

She snorted.

'One of nature's doormats. A good nurse, mind. You know to let your patient have a moan when she needs one. Bet you don't know when to tell me to shut up and be grateful, though. You let those two step-daughters of yours walk all over you.'

'They're my daughters,' I told her, absently wiping dust from the mantelpiece.

'Gave birth to 'em, did you? Carried them for nine

months and cussed out the doctors while they came into the world?'

I put down my duster.

'*They're my daughters.*'

We looked at each other in surprise. Then she chuckled.

'You've got *some* blood in your veins, then. Still, at home on *Lundi Gras* . . . definitely one of nature's doormats. But I'm going to transform you, my dear.'

'What—'

Her eyes were like rain-washed berries in her wrinkled brown face.

'Go to the closet,' she ordered.

I opened an ornate wooden door, looked inside, took a breath.

'You like it?' she demanded, sitting up in bed and straining to see my expression.

'It's—oh, it's just . . .'

Hanging on a padded hanger was a crimson dress: long bell-sleeves, a low neck, a fitted bodice, a long, flared skirt. Ruffles trailed around the *décolletage*, across the bodice and down, down—a dress for a princess, for a queen, accompanied by a red sequinned Carnival mask and crimson silk heels.

'Put it on,' Hazel commanded.

'I'm too old.'

'Rubbish. Put it on.'

'I'm thirty-eight years old, and I *can't wear that dress*.'

'Horseshit. You can, and you will. Put it *on*.'

'I—'

'I used to be a costumier,' said Hazel. 'Sewed for the finest Krewes of the city.' She held up her ruined hands. 'I dressed the Parade Kings and Queens every year for twenty-three years straight, till my joints got too bad, more'n ten years ago. That's one of the last three dresses I made, and it's waited a long time. *Age is nothing.* I'm seventy-three years old and I'm still not done. Thirty-eight's just getting started. Do as you're told, Ella, and damn well put — it — on.'

The cool silk made my skin shiver. My bra showed in back, so I tossed it recklessly away, to lie grey and discouraged in a corner. I shook my hair loose; I tied on the mask. The shoes held my feet like jewels. I showed myself to Hazel.

'Ah,' she sighed, her face bright with satisfaction.

'How does it — ?'

'There's a mirror on the closet door.'

I opened the door and looked, and looked, and looked.

'Old Hollywood,' said Hazel, smiling. 'So. *Now* are you going out?'

'Yes,' I said.

I stepped into colour, smell, noise, freedom, and was instantly lost; but I didn't care. I felt found. I floated lightly on the tide of people, and I was by the kerb as a Spanish Galleon sailed round the street corner. On the deck stood a man in black doublet and hose, a white lace ruff, a pointed beard beneath a black leather mask. As he tossed doubloons into the crowd, he saw me.

At his command, the float came to a slow halt, and he leapt down. I tried to hide, but he thrust through the crowd, found me, took my hand. The skin of his palm was warm and rough.

'Come aboard,' he invited.

'I can't.'

'Why not?'

'Because — because —'

I had no idea who he was, how old he was, what he

looked like. But my hand rested in his, our bodies whispering to each other, even as we tripped and stumbled over our tongues.

'Please,' he said. 'We're not supposed to stop, so I'm already in trouble. But it's worth it if you'll come with me.'

His hand was so warm, so dry.

'Yes,' I said.

We sailed the streets, throwing coins, laughing, talking. He couldn't tell me his name –Krewe memberships were still secret then — and I refused to share mine. He called me Isabella; I called him Vasquez. And we talked, oh, how we talked; talked as if we'd starved for it all our lives.

Finally, we docked at Parade's End.

'I have to go,' I said.

He stroked my wrist shyly with his fingertips. His touch was melting, paralysing.

'Can I see you again? Please?'

'How — ? I don't know your name.'

'Be at Fat Tuesday tomorrow and I'll find you.'

He kissed the inside of my wrist. Something inside me caught fire.

'Yes,' I said.

Fat Tuesday dawned. Beth and Cindy shimmied into their costumes.

'D'you know,' said Beth discontentedly, 'the parade *stopped* yesterday because some guy wanted a spectator up on his float.'

'He should have picked you, Bethie,' said Cindy. 'It was a ship, Mom. Beth would have looked perfect.'

'You both look perfect now,' I said sincerely.

'Good.' She glanced at the ball dresses hanging on the

door: gold and glimmer for Cindy, silver and shimmer for Beth. 'We can't go to the balls without invitations.'

'You'll be asked,' I said, smiling.

'Oh, *Mom*,' said Beth. 'You've been out of the game too long, you don't know how it works . . .' She frowned into the mirror. 'I need a different mask. Can I borrow some money?'

'Of course,' I said.

Beth was already rummaging in my wallet. 'I'm taking ten dollars, all right? Oh, hang on—Cindy wanted silver stockings—those ones we saw, remember? Twenty should be enough. We'll see you later, okay?'

'Yes,' I said.

The door had hardly closed before I heard Hazel thumping; her hearing was supernatural, I thought, or else there was no soundproofing. She was in her chair this time, damaged hands resting cautiously on her stick.

'You look better,' she complimented me. 'Less dead. You met someone, didn't you? About time, too. You already wasted twenty years. The next twenty have to count for double.'

'They were not wasted!' I protested. 'I was bringing up my daughters!'

'Hmmph.'

'Don't be mean about my children, Hazel . . .'

'Oh, be quiet.' Her eyes twinkled. 'Look in the closet.'

An empire-line column of soft green taffeta, slit to the hips and trimmed with old-gold ribbon. Filmy, sequinned wings, outrageously wide and feather-light; a mask crusted with crystals and topped with peacock feathers; sandals too delicate to be worn more than once. A dress to make Titania weep. I felt tears come to my eyes.

'Why are you doing this for me?' I asked.

Hazel smiled to herself.

'Every woman needs a little help sometimes,' she said. 'Don't even think about ruining the line with those ghastly underpants. You could hide them under the red frock, but not this one. And leave that dreadful thing you call a brassiere as well.'

'But—'

'Trust me, you're better off naked than wearing *them*. Get dressed. And then . . .' she held out a little box.

'What's in there?' I asked, feeling taffeta caress me.

'Make-up. I can't do it for you, *these* damn things—' she shook her hands and winced '—are no use, so you'll have to do what I tell you. Exactly what I tell you, mind you.'

'Will it show under the mask?'

'You think we're going to paint your *face*?'

An hour later, under Hazel's direction, my body bloomed with leaves and flowers, winding and winding around my limbs, my chest, my neck. I looked beautiful, but eerie, faerie; I looked transformed.

Hazel chuckled to herself.

'Of course, what I *should* have done is make that dress without a bodice, and got you to paint your tits,' she said. 'Far too pretty to keep under wraps. Never mind. Now, about tonight's ball. He'll offer; don't you dare turn him down.'

'Who are you talking about?'

'You know perfectly well,' she said severely. 'Promise me you'll accept?'

'Yes,' I said.

I'll find you, he'd said, but how could he, in this ocean of humanity? He didn't even know what I looked like. Nevertheless, my stomach was full of butterflies.

On Bourbon Street, I smelled the Mississippi on the breeze. The costumes here were wilder, more risqué; I saw women with their breasts bared, one painted with a *trompe l'oeil* Wall Street suit, red suspenders and striped shirt, stalking naked down the street with her head held high. I remembered Hazel's words—*I should have got you to paint your tits*—and shivered.

How could they do it? How could they be so exposed, their bodies bare while their faces hid behind a mask?

But a part of me envied them their freedom.

Of course, even then no-one could parade through the *Quartier*, so I made my way to Canal Street. How could Hazel have known the parades that day were Faerie-themed? My costume could have come straight from one of the floats that drifted through the warm, heavy air. Woodland scenes, court scenes, nymphs reclining by water; seven beautiful girls and seven beautiful boys going down to hell with chains around their necks.

And then—a gigantic ass's head, ears flapping in the breeze, a long tongue poured between vast yellow teeth to form a carpet, the King of the Faeries on a filigree throne. Next to him, Titania's vacant place. This time I didn't wait to be fetched from the crowd.

'I thought each Krewe only paraded once,' I said.

'We're rule-breakers,' he said gravely. 'Hadn't you noticed?'

As I took my place, he kissed me, a brush of his lips against my ear that made my pulse race. We were supposed to throw coins to the crowd, but we didn't. Instead two woodland sylphs took over, while we devoured the air between us, ravenous for each other's words.

'But how did you know?' I asked. 'How did you find me?'

His eyes roamed over me; it felt like being touched.

'How did *you* know?' he asked. 'That frock . . . that mask . . . that *make-up* . . .' he sighed.

'What's wrong?'

'I wish we could be alone,' he said simply. 'I want to see if you're painted like that all over. That sounds very forward, I wouldn't dare say it without the mask, but it's true.'

I didn't know how to answer.

'Come to the ball tonight,' he said, offering a scalloped card. Our fingers touched.

'Say you'll be there,' he said. 'Please, Titania.'

'Yesterday you called me Isabella.'

'Because you won't tell me who you are really.'

A widow of twenty years with two grown-up children, closer to forty than thirty.

'You wouldn't want to know,' I said.

'I do, but I'll wait — I just have to see you again — will you come to the ball?'

Don't you dare turn him down. Hazel could have been standing beside me.

'Yes,' I said.

I was only just in time for Beth and Cindy. Of course, they'd been offered invitations too. Meekly, I helped them dress. But I was all alive inside, wondering what Hazel had planned. When the summons came, I took cookies and milk.

'These aren't bad,' Hazel said, pleased. 'And in return . . .'

As I went to the closet, she caught my wrist. Her touch was light, her poor, arthritic fingers had no traction, but she had me captured.

'This one takes courage,' she told me.

'All right . . .'

'I mean it. You open that door, you're putting it on. You hear?'

I was mystified, and afraid, and desperately curious.

'Yes,' I said, and opened the door.

'You need talcum powder,' said Hazel calmly. 'Don't shake your head, Ella. It's going on.'

'I won't, I *can't*, I—'

She held the talcum out.

'Turn it inside out and shake this over it. Then turn it right-side out again. Take your time, it's not something to rush. And don't roll it up, it's not hosiery. Just step into it. Oh, don't *cry*. It'll be astounding.'

I wiped tears off my face.

'Don't cry,' Hazel repeated, and touched me under the chin. 'Trust me.'

I took the cold, heavy, slippery, strange-smelling *thing* into the tiny bathroom and stripped naked, not daring to meet my own gaze. I turned it inside out and shook talcum all over it, then turned it right-side out again.

It looked like nothing I'd ever seen.

'Damn it,' I wailed, and stepped into it, slowly, as she told me to, and felt it slither over me, and pulled the zipper smoothly up in back.

And then . . .

. . . then, the black rubber catsuit held me in a cool, firm embrace. It sculpted and lifted, smoothed and firmed; it clung to every inch of my skin; it *was* my skin, my new skin, my skin I could wear outdoors. I looked in the mirror, and laughed out loud.

'Do you see?' said Hazel, her eyes blackbird-bright. '*Cher* Ella, do you see?'

It was a revelation. He could get close, but he couldn't

touch; he'd see part of me, but he could only caress my smooth outer shell. I was hiding in plain sight.

'*Yes*,' I said.

Crowds parted as I walked down the street, tall in shiny black heels. The doorman bowed. As I entered the ball-room, a respectful silence fell.

He was waiting by the long windows overlooking the river, wearing skin-tight white lycra, like a ballet dancer. I saw him catch his breath. This time we barely spoke, we just twined closely together and danced; but a photographer, moving among the couples, stopped and snapped a shot of us.

'You're going to have to dance every dance with me,' he said at last.

'Why?' I asked, knowing the answer.

'Because,' he said, 'because, because . . . because this damn costume doesn't hide a thing, and if I let you go, all New Orleans will see I've got the most unconquerable hard-on of my life . . . don't laugh, I'm serious . . .'

'I'm laughing because I'm nervous. It's been so long . . .'

'How long?'

'Twenty years.'

He stopped dancing. 'Are you—you're not—have I got this all wrong, do you—um—prefer—'

I laughed.

'Absolutely not.'

'Then—' He stroked my cheek. 'Did something *happen*? To make you—'

'No, no, no,' I said. 'Nothing like that. It was just—circumstances.'

'And now?'

'And now I'm on fire,' I admitted, with a sob.

'Oh, God.' his voice was hoarse. 'Come with me, I have a room. Please.'

'I can't take this costume off.'

'Then leave it on. Just—let me make love to you. *Please*.'

'Yes,' I said.

Cotton sheets and a gold brocade cover, but I was cocooned in my skin, my slick black second skin. He stroked me everywhere, but he could only touch my face, my hands, my feet, and—somewhere else. There was a second zipper, you see; a modesty fastening, they call them, although I never felt more immodest in my life than when he—

His fingers, stroking and caressing.

His breath hot on my cheek.

His erection, hot and alive under my touch.

His voice, begging me to stop, telling me it was too much, he just couldn't wait if I—

His hands, stopping me from touching him because I couldn't stop myself.

And then he was inside my skin, inside my body, and when we screamed aloud in sheer wild ecstasy, I thought we'd bring the ceiling down.

I awoke at quarter to twelve. Beth and Cindy—the room left cluttered and littered—my clothes in a heap on Hazel's floor.

'I have to go,' I said.

'Wait,' he said, trying to hold me. 'Mardi Gras ends at midnight.'

'That's why I need to go.'

'Stay. Please.'

'I can't.'

'Why not?'

'Tomorrow everything's real again. I can't be here when that happens.'

'Yes, you can.' He stroked my face. 'Stay with me. I want to wake up tomorrow and find you here. I want to peel you out of that suit and see you properly naked. This isn't the end; it can't be. Please.'

'It's late, I need to go—'

His eyes were intense in the dim light.

'Marry me,' he begged suddenly.

'*What*?'

'Marry me.' He slid out of bed and knelt at my feet. 'I'm serious. I've never felt this way in my life. Marry me.'

'I can't! I have a family—'

'You're already married?'

'No, no, widowed, but—'

He began to kiss me. My body was melting; my will was dissolving; I felt the universe hold its breath.

I closed my eyes, and pushed him away.

'*No*,' I said.

I ran barefoot from the room.

Why? Well, why do you think?

Lots of reasons. Because it was insane. Because I hadn't taken a risk for twenty years. Because the last time I got married, my husband was dead within a year. Most of all, because I was afraid, when the mask came off, he'd see me and think, *oh, shit* . . .

The newspaper article? You have a copy? I haven't seen it since—may I—oh—oh my—

KREWE MEMBER BREAKS CODE,
SEEKS LOVE

The King of the Krewe of Olde Stratford broke with strict tradition last night by publicly revealing his identity in a bid to find the mysterious lady he danced with at the Lundi Gras Krewe Ball.

Brandan Orlando, 33, says he is 'completely unconcerned' about his expulsion and only wants to find the lady (right). 'She's amazing,' he said. 'I'd do anything to find her. Please—if you're reading this—please get in touch.'

Mr Orlando's lady friend may care to consider that he's the owner of Orlando Publishing Ltd, and worth an estimated $3.9m. She can contact Mr Orlando via our offices, or through the PO Box detailed below.

He was handsome and kind-looking, with a lovely smile. And that *other* picture . . .

The woman in the photograph was beautiful, powerful, in control. No wonder he fell in love with her. But I'd only borrowed her skin for a few brief hours. I put the paper down.

'Look, Beth,' said Cindy. 'It's that couple we saw at the ball. Wow, he's *rich* . . .'

'She's got some nerve,' said Beth, 'wearing that slutty costume. Don't you think, Mom? Mom? Are you all right?'

'I'm sorry?'

'Are you all right, I said?'

'Yes,' I said.

Back in Delacroix, everything cold and grey now. My

body wouldn't go back to sleep; I woke in the night wanting, yearning. This was how it would be from now on. I'd be the slave of these two beautiful, thoughtless girls until the day someone married them; and then I'd be nothing to anyone any more, and I'd live alone until I died.

A rainy afternoon. Cindy was on the phone, Beth was watching television. I was cleaning the kitchen, a mountain of ironing to do afterwards. I barely looked up when I heard the gate. I went to the door, dishcloth in hand.

Standing in the doorway was Brandan. I bit my tongue in shock.

'Hello,' he said, trying to smile.

I dropped the dishcloth.

'I . . .' he held out a wet paper bag. 'I think I have your shoes.'

The wicked black stilettos, left behind so I could run faster. I looked at them wordlessly.

'It is you, isn't it?' he pleaded. 'I've been looking for you for weeks — I went to every hotel and boarding house in New Orleans, trying to find someone who knew you. I met this amazing old woman, Hazel. She told me she'd kept those dresses for the right person . . . please, talk to me, tell me it's you . . .' His voice broke. 'Oh, God, I don't even know your name.'

'It's Ella,' I said, finding my voice at last. 'My name's Ella Jenkins, and I'm an ordinary, boring, *thirty-eight-year-old* housewife with two grown-up daughters. I'm the dullest person I know, even Hazel called me one of nature's doormats. I'm sorry, this is why I ran away, it was so much fun being someone else for a while, but that was just for Mardi Gras —'

He kissed me then, and left my heart leaping. I had to press hard on my chest to keep it in.

'Shhh,' he told me. 'Please, Ella, darling Ella, shut up. I *love you*. I've thought about no-one else since I met you. You're the most incredible, heart-shaking thing that's ever, ever happened to me, and I know this is crazy, and I just don't care.' He knelt at my feet. 'If you don't want to marry me, just give me a year and a day. At the end of it, if you're not happy, you can leave. Or you can marry me now and take half of everything I own, I'll risk it. I just want you to give us a chance. Please, Ella, say yes.'

'What's going on?' Beth wandered onto the porch, wrinkling her nose at the rain. 'Who's this guy? Cindy, get out here, there's something weird happening—'

'This is Brandan,' I said, dazedly. 'He wants me to marry him.'

'*Marry* him—Mom, that's nuts, you've never met him before—'

'Actually, I have,' I said.

Cindy arrived, holding the cordless phone she'd begged for.

'I've called the police,' she told Brandan. 'Don't worry, Mom, we'll get rid of him.'

Brandan ignored her.

'Come with me,' he said. 'We'll talk on the way.'

'I—I don't have any shoes on.'

He held out the stilettos.

'If that's the only thing stopping you . . .'

'Yes!' I said, laughing. 'Yes, yes, yes, yes, *yes!*'

And I put on those black stilettos, took his hand, and ran away with him into the rain.

Interview #9

—Henry Reynolds
Baton Rouge, Louisiana

YOU KNOW HOW Baton Rouge got its name, right? Back in the seventeenth century, this French explorer came up the Mississippi, rounded a bend in the water and found this huge cedar tree with dead fish and animals nailed to it. He called it the Red Stick. *Baton Rouge.*

Me, I always wondered about that. That explorer was a good Christian, same as we are, he could see that Red Stick for what it was. But it still musta got into his head, because when it came time to name that settlement they founded . . .

Course, I ain't educated the way you are. I'm just a retired Louisiana cop, never got past high school, and I ain't ashamed of that, neither. But I reckon I can tell you a tale to make you wonder if that explorer mighta been onto something, when he decided to call his brand new settlement after that Red Stick, that offering to the Devil himself.

There was three of us — me, Mike Stone and Randy Lewis — been hunting this guy for days. Robaire Lebrun; a tragic excuse for a man. Sold drugs, pimped his woman, beat his momma; an all-round blot on society. Well, now he'd shot some other piece of trash, and we was coming after him for Murder One.

We chased him, and we lost him, and we found him, and we chased him again. He ran like a frightened rabbit; but we chased him right across town, on foot I might add, which tells you how bad we wanted him. Finally had him pinned in the alley down the back of Peachtree Street.

We'd done all the running we could stand that day, and we was hot and tired and thirsty. I took out my piece.

'Robaire, I am just about done chasing your sorry self! Don't you make me shoot you now.'

He looked at us wild-eyed, chest heaving, hands scrabbling. Probably high on something; he mostly was. And then, darn if he didn't find an unlocked door and dash inside.

'Go around the front,' gasped Mike. 'I'll take back.'

It was July, and we was sweating like hogs. Mike opened the door and snuck inside. Randy and I ran back down the alley, wiping our foreheads, counting doors, round to the sidewalk to find the fifth building, which turned out to be a restaurant. The afternoon sun was like a poke in the eye.

'There he is,' I gasped, pointing. 'Look!'

He was walking out of that restaurant like he didn't have a care in the world.

'Robaire!' I shouted. 'Robaire Lebrun!'

He didn't even flinch, just kept right on rolling. The sun made my eyes water, but we both saw it — clear as day — he turned towards the restaurant — *reached into his pocket* — and started back.

No *way* was he walking back in there and shooting his way outta trouble; not with my friend and fellow officer inside. I figured I had no choice.

So I shot him.

❧

How did it feel? Dear Lord, how the — how d'you think it felt? Not good, okay? The Good Book tells us, *Thou Shalt Not Kill*, and a sin that grave's a heavy burden. But what you don't realise — because it's the job of folks like me to fix it so you don't *have* to realise — is we are in a *war* out there. And in wars, people die. Was Robaire's life worth the lives of the restaurant customers? Not a chance. So yeah, I shot to kill, you bet. Clean shot, straight to the heart; dropped him like a sack of potatoes.

Robaire Lebrun, lying on the sidewalk in a pool of his own blood. Mike and I had him covered just in case, but we was pretty tarnation sure he was dead. Crowd starts to gather. Randy gets on the radio and calls it in. We keep our pieces trained on him and listen to the pretty girl in Dispatch taking notes.

'Ambulance required, repeat, ambulance required. Suspect has been shot resisting arrest. Yes, m'am, that's right, shot resisting arrest. We had cause to believe he was about to open fire on a crowded restaurant. Robaire Lebrun, African American male, five seven tall, slender build . . .'

Mike and I start to feel uneasy.

'We're outside the Bubbling Saucepan Diner on Peachtree Street. Crowd is gathering, repeat, crowd is gathering.' Code for *we shot a black guy, get here quick.* 'Request back-up . . .'

'Looks bigger'n five, seven,' murmured Mike.

'Says five, seven on the rap sheet,' I murmured back.

'Ain't skinny neither. And Robaire was wearin' a T-shirt. This guy's wearing a dress shirt.'

We stared at each other.

Let's be clear. We saw a man who broadly matched the description of our suspect come out of the location we knew he was in and make a threatening gesture, and we reacted accordingly. The death of Mr Daniel Arbuckle was a tragic mistake. He was a decent man and a credit to his community—a little forgetfulness about restaurant bills aside—who happened to be in the wrong place at the wrong time. But that's the nature of the war we're engaged in. We were exonerated before a disciplinary board and by the coroner.

I can see from your face the thoughts you're entertaining. Well, I recommend you put those thoughts right back out on the doorstep. Yes, Mr Arbuckle wasn't the first man I shot in the line of duty. In point of fact, he was the third. And yes, as it happened, all three of them were black. You know what that means? It means *I am a cop.*

You know how many drug dealers I put away? How many pimps? How many whores? How many robbers and wife-beaters and carjackers?

Know how many of 'em was white?

So we went through the disciplinary, not the first for any of us. We went to church and asked forgiveness, and prayed for the soul of Mr Arbuckle. We put it behind us. That's what you have to do, the only way to live with it. We eventually got Robaire, and sent him down for fifteen to twenty. We went on fighting the good fight. Summer turned to Fall, and the rains started coming in.

And then, one night . . .

I'd seen this girl—this woman—at the inquest. There was a million reasons why I shouldn't have been looking.

She sat by the family of Mr Arbuckle, and Lord knows we had little enough to say to each other. I was far too old and fat and bald for her; and I was kind of seeing Marilena from the traffic division besides. But I swear, when I laid eyes on her . . . she was like a poem set to Blues music.

She was the colour of sweet chocolate, and she had kind of a beige-coloured dress — I don't know the proper name for it — but she wore it like it was her skin. Her hair curled like ribbons on a jeweller's box, long black ribbons held back from her face with clips like butterflies. She wasn't skinny the way the girls all seem to be nowadays, she was curvy and ripe and — ah, hell, she was *womanly,* meaning she reminded me I was a man, and that's as dainty as I know how to say it. I stole glances at her whenever I could, while the Medical Examiner droned, and Mr Arbuckle sat stiff and straight as if he'd died there, and Mrs Arbuckle's mother wept into a tissue.

And when I was in the witness box, I saw her watching me.

I admit I sucked my gut in, stood a little straighter. I felt dumb doing it, but as I live and breathe, she truly was that luscious. She made even a middle-aged man who oughta know better wish he was young and sinful again.

'So, Officer Reynolds, you both saw Mr Arbuckle reach inside his jacket, is that your statement?' prompted the ME, and I dragged my attention away from her mouth and back to the business at hand. But I could feel her eyes on me the whole time.

I admit I was more'n a little flustered when I finally got down off of the stand. To be perfectly honest, it felt like she couldn't wait to get her hands on me.

When I got back on duty, I looked through the Arbuckle file for any clues about who she might be. Arbuckle had a sister, but it wasn't her — nice girl, but nothing like that siren who'd been haunting my dreams. Wasn't his girlfriend neither — she was a pretty redhead from Pennsylvania. Certainly wasn't his mother. Didn't seem to be any part of his extended family. I asked around, but nobody else even remembered her — nobody except Mike and Randy, and believe me, they'd noticed her too.

I guess some dumb-ass part of me was looking out for her for a while, wondering if she'd show up at the station, needing a little advice from the officer she'd seen at the inquest. But she never showed.

Not until that Godforsaken night.

Marilena and I had drifted apart, nothing dramatic, it just fizzled, so I was home alone. I was watching the game and drinking the fourth beer of the night when the doorbell rang. A cop's gotta be careful, so I checked out the kitchen window first.

The rain was coming down heavy, and she was stood beneath the porch light wearing a black leather coat and long black leather boots. The rain clung to her hair like diamonds. I sucked in my breath. My hand was right on the lock, and I must confess it was trembling a little.

Then, something; that tickle of intuition . . .

'Can I help you?' I asked instead, through the door.

'Officer Reynolds?' She didn't sound local; more kinda Bajan, I guess. A voice that could read from the phone book and make it sound like an invitation.

'Yeah,' I said cautiously.

'I would like to come in, please.'

'Would you, now?' That tickle becoming something stronger. I wished I'd got my gun. I could see it lying by the chair, but I wanted to stay where I could see her.

'Is that a problem?'

'I saw you at the inquest,' I said, stalling.

'And I saw you.' She smiled widely. 'I *remembered* you. If it's convenient, I'd like to talk to you about that day. There's . . . something I'd like to discuss with you.'

That black leather coat was smooth and slick, the kind of garment you see a woman wearing and automatically start thinking how much you'd like to take it off again. It fit her as closely as if she was the creature it came from. I swallowed.

'So,' she continued. 'May I come in?'

No, I don't know how I knew. I just — *knew*. You know? Call it — cop's instinct.

'I don't think so,' I said, trying to think. I wanted my gun more than I'd ever wanted anything in my life.

'There's something we need to discuss.'

'What would that be?'

She put one hand on her hip, and smiled.

'You ain't here for that.'

'How do you know?'

'Cuz I'm a cop,' I growled. 'I'm dumb, but I'm not that dumb. You've got better things to do with your evening than seduce a fat middle-aged redneck like me.'

Her laugh was like music. They do say the Devil has all the best tunes.

'Very well, Officer Reynolds. We need to talk — about justice.'

Keep her talking — wait for inspiration — damn it, what the hell am I gonna do?

'Justice is for the courts,' I tried.

She shook her head.

'No, Officer Reynolds, that is the *law*.' It felt like she was looking right at me through the wooden door. 'The law's powerful, of course; Mr Arbuckle's dead because of the law. It's amazing what you can accomplish when you have a gun, isn't it?'

'I got the right to bear arms.'

'Do you have the right to kill?'

'When I have to.'

'And did you have to kill Mr Arbuckle?'

'Ma'am, I'm sorry for what happened, but I had *cause,* you heard what the—'

'You didn't shoot him because you thought he was dangerous, did you? You tell yourself that, but you know in your heart it's not true. You shot him because you were hot and thirsty, and a black man made you chase him and you wanted to get your own back. You couldn't even be sure it was him. You were like a man coming home and kicking his dog off the porch because he's had a fight with his boss.'

'That's not true,' I croaked. At that moment, I reckon my throat musta been the only dry spot in the city. If I'd been thinking clearly, I'd have wondered how we could even hear each other over the rain.

'Isn't it?'

I tried to answer, couldn't get the words out. Felt like my hand was glued to the lock.

'This is getting boring.' She was fumbling with her belt, and the dumbest, horniest part of me was still secretly hoping she was just some gorgeous maniac who got off on bad men doing bad things, and beneath that coat, she'd have nothing more dangerous than her own naked self. The coat fell open.

'The thing is,' she continued, as she took one of those wicked little fire-devils off her belt and held it in her hand. 'Since you won't let me come in, I do believe I'll have to blow your house up.'

Instinct's a dangerous dog to let off the leash. I've seen *instinct* make people run onto guns, jump off buildings, dash in front of traffic, gut themselves climbing razor-wire. But sometimes that dog just gets away from you; and sometimes that dog knows exactly what he's doing.

I shot through my house like a bullet from a gun—or like a crude but adequate home-made explosive device through a kitchen window. I didn't collect my piece, I didn't grab my car keys, I didn't get my wallet, and I certainly didn't stop to worry that I was wearing nothing but shorts and a bathrobe, no shoes, even. That's why I'm still alive to tell this story.

That old black dog, Instinct, dragged me out the back door, across the yard and down the sidewalk, away from the *boom* as the bomb went off, away from the flames as my modest little brick-built home burned to the ground. It pulled me to the end of the street with my bathrobe flapping loose, like an escaped mental patient. Then it kinda ran outta steam and I stood there letting the rain soak me to the skin, while Instinct nosed around the trash-cans and we both wondered what to do next.

I thought as fast as I could. She'd found me, don't know how hard she'd had to try, but she'd found me. She'd blown up my house without hesitation or remorse. She'd given me no second chance.

She'd had two more of those babies on her belt.

And then Instinct was back in charge, pulling on the leash, and I was running through wet streets in my bare feet towards Randy's house.

Randy had this Gulf Coast-style cottage, something his ex-wife Marybelle had been crazy for. Randy wasn't all that keen, but he loved Marybelle so he went along with it, and when she ran off with a trucker from Houston, he never got around to selling up and buying something more masculine. I looked around in case *she'd* got there first—which, given my age, weight and lack of transportation or footwear, seemed highly possible—but there was no sign of her, and all the cars on the street were familiar and empty. I staggered up the porch and banged on the door.

That little pause you always get when a cop gets an unexpected caller, and then Randy dragged me in over the threshold.

'Henry, what the—'

I could hardly speak.

'That woman,' I managed at last.

'*Marilena?*'

'From the inquest—*you* know the one I mean.'

He looked at my soaking bathrobe.

'Are you serious? That beautiful thing who gave us all the glad-eye?' He whistled. 'You lucky, *lucky* bastard. But what you doing *here* if—'

'She blew up my house,' I managed, finally getting my breath. 'She'll come for you next . . .'

He got it instantly. He pushed aside the muslin Marybelle left on the screen door and peered out.

And there she was, standing under the street lamp like she'd been there all along, rain streaming off her coat, hair like ribbons, and a smile exactly halfway between provocation and threat. There were tears in the coat and dust in the creases, and blood trickled down the curve of her cheek. When she wiped it away, I saw half one sleeve was missing, and her arm was blistered.

'Officer Lewis?' The rain was so bad it was like God had a bucket and was pouring it out over us, but we heard every word clear as a bell. 'Good evening.'

'You got your piece?' I hissed.

Randy shook his head.

'Tell me where. I'll go.'

'Nightstand, in the—'

She reached beneath her coat and held up her hand. Devil-baby Number Two was in it.

'I'd advise you both to stay by the door,' she said gravely. 'I will know if either of you move.'

And God help me, we both believed her. Instinct was in charge, and he swore blind we needed to be scared, because her dog was bigger than either of ours; she was smarter and faster and stronger, and she had the upper hand. She'd given all of us that look in the witness box and we were men and men are dumb-ass optimists, so we'd all looked for her, and come up empty. But she'd found us like it was nothing at all.

'What do you want?' Randy asked.

When she smiled, we saw her white, sharp teeth.

'I want to come in,' she said. 'To talk to you.'

'About Mr Arbuckle?' asked Randy warily.

'About Mr Daniel Arbuckle, and about Mr Theodore Santiago. I wonder if you gentlemen can tell me what these names have in common?'

Again the dog's advice, I inched away from the doorway.

'Don't,' she said. 'Don't do that, Officer Reynolds.'

I stopped.

'They're both—ah—men of colour,' said Randy.

'Indeed. Tell me, Officer Reynolds. Is it true your father was a Klansman?'

We looked at each other.

Yeah, as it happens, she was right. My daddy was a Klansman, my granddaddy too. And I ain't ashamed of that, no sir. I'm proud of my heritage and of my ancestors. Some of what they did was wrong, but I reckon some of what all of our parents did was wrong. *Honour thy father and mother*, that's what we're all commanded to do. I may not agree with every choice they made, but I certainly won't disrespect them to a stranger.

But I'll tell you again, and this is all I'll say on that subject; I am a *cop*. For thirty-one years I protected, and I served. Want to know who I protected? Those very same black people you got such a look on your face about. I went into their parts of town, walked those mean streets, arrested the bad elements in their communities. I spent my working career watching over the black people of Baton Rouge. What would your friends back up in Washington State make of that? How do y'all like them apples, huh?

Randy, bless his heart, spoke up for me.

'Henry's a good man. His daddy mighta made some mistakes, but this is America, we can all rise above our past. Ma'am, if you're dissatisfied with an officer of the law, you can make your complaint to—'

'This isn't about the *law*,' she said scornfully. 'Henry understands. Don't you, Henry?'

Randy wiped sweat off his nose. He always sweated when he got nervous. I did stake-out with him once, three shifts of twelve hours straight watching a crack-house. Randy never had to pee once.

'Mr Santiago was shot resisting arrest.'

'How much resistance can a man put up when he's making love to the woman he's stone crazy about? He was in bed with her when you found him, wasn't he? Oh, there was a gun in the nightstand, but he wasn't reaching for it, was he? You just decided he deserved to die.'

My turn to paddle Randy's canoe.

'Ma'am, *we* shot him, both of us, because he was dangerous. He was a *dealer*, he ran a crack house—'

35

'But you didn't shoot him because he was a drug dealer. You did it because of his girlfriend. You killed a black man because he was sleeping with a white woman. Officer Lewis, you shot him first, through the back of his ribcage and into his heart, and that shot killed him. Henry, you came in afterwards and put one in the back of his head, just to make sure. You didn't even know she was underneath him until you heard her screaming.'

I watched my thoughts scrolling past the space behind Randy's eyes.

How does she know all this?

Forget about that, just keep her talking.

Randy cleared his throat, his voice as careful as if he was proposing. 'Ma'am, may I ask if this — this business is personal to you?'

'*Personal.* Hmm. As in, *pertaining to a particular person?* Yes, Officer Lewis, I'd say this is personal.'

'Mr Santiago was a relative?' Trying to build a rapport. To remind her she was human. Randy knew the drill same as I did.

'Oh, if you look hard enough, we're all relatives. I suppose you could say I'm acting on behalf of someone for whom it's personal.' She sighed, and inspected the blisters on her forearm. 'Something tells me you're not going to let me in.'

'Ma'am, if I accidentally did harm to someone in your family then I truly do apologise, but you have to understand—'

That laugh again, beautiful the way a wolf's beautiful when it howls to the moon.

'And I *truly do apologise* for what I did to Henry's house. Likewise for what I'm about to do to yours. But *you* have to understand some things are inevitable. You men with your guns and your badges, you try to tame the beast, kill it with laws and *civilisation*. But sometimes, the beast has to fight back. Just to remind you a gun will only get you so far.'

We saw the light move along her leather-clad arm as she made the throw.

And once again I was running, Randy running too, both of us pulled by that wild dog, Instinct. My legs were like jelly, but Instinct didn't care. Randy and I lit outta that house just as the *boom* of the explosion hit. A plank of burning wood hit my head and set fire to the little bits of hair I had left. The smell of burning hair's disgusting. Specially when it's your own.

Randy was wearing sweats and a T-shirt. By sheer good luck he had the keys to his flatbed in his pocket.

'Where's Mike?' he demanded as he accelerated down the street.

'Out at the mud hut.'

'Again? He ain't with that chick he was seeing?'

I squeezed about a pint of water outta the sleeve of my bathrobe. 'Mike likes it in the Bayou.'

'I swear, that man's a gator at heart.'

'Good, cuz we're gonna need a gator to take *her* on.'

The tires squealed as we turned the corner.

'Who d'you think she is?' asked Randy after a minute. 'You think she's a pro?'

I laughed. Weren't no way she was a pro. We get 'em, same as any big city, but hit-men almost always work for gangs and dealers, which means they mostly just kill bangers and dealers, and other hit-men. Plus, they're always men. Beautiful women have just one use in Gang-land, and it don't involve a whole lotta personal freedom.

'No,' I said. 'She ain't a pro.'

'So who *is* she?'

'Randy, I don't know.' I knew what I thought, but I didn't want to say it out loud.

'You reckon she'll find us out there?'

'She'll find us.'

'But how? That little shack's just about built outta sticks and straw. It ain't on any map I've seen. Remember that fishing trip Mike made us all take that time? Hell, there ain't even a road!'

'She'll find us,' I repeated. I squeezed the other sleeve, got another pint of water out.

Randy opened his mouth to say something, then closed it again.

We picked splinters of wood out of our skin and clothes as we drove.

Why'd we run for the Bayou? Good question. Why Mike's sorry little shack, when we was both serving officers who coulda gone to any station in town, raised the roof and turned the troops loose on that beautiful hellion who was hunting us down? It made no sense at all. But we weren't thinking like cops any more. We was barely thinking at all. Instinct had slipped its leash.

But there's another answer, one I ain't never dared say out loud before now. America's a Christian land: one nation, united under God, whose son Jesus died for our sins. But here in Louisiana, we got this *other* thing. It came outta the slave quarters, and it's something we ain't never civilised away, no matter how many tax dollars goes into trying, and we all act like it's charming and touristy, but it ain't. There's the Voodoo Queens who charm the snakes, and the women who pray to the spirit of Marie Laveau, and the *Loup-Garou* who prowls the swamps and steals children . . .

I think we ran for the Bayou because she put a spell on us.

As God's my witness, you ain't *never* seen blackness like the Lousiana Bayou by night. No street lights, no house lights, no firelight, no nothing. When the rain's coming down in sheets, not even the stars keep you company. Just me, Randy and a torch whose batteries we weren't too confident of. Walking away from Randy's flatbed, rags around my feet instead of shoes, was just about the hardest thing I'd ever done. Felt like walking back in time, back to the days of the ole Red Stick.

That nasty little shack of Mike's looked even worse than we'd remembered. It was kinda slouched up against an inlet of stagnant water, no glass, just wooden shutters, just barely holding together, most of it rotten and damp. Mike said it was *simple*. Yeah, and your dog defecating on the rug is *natural*. We'd spent three days there once. It was supposed to be a week, but we ran outta beer, and Randy and I couldn't stand it sober. We banged on the door and hoped it wouldn't fall down.

A pause, and then Mike dragged the door open. He stared in disbelief.

'What the Sam Hill are y'all—'

'Let us in,' gasped Randy. ''fore the gators get us.'

'There ain't no gators now, they hunt at dusk—y'all wanna tell me what this is about? Henry, forgive me—there a reason you wearing a bathrobe?'

We staggered over the threshold. It smelled like the Bayou, and the fish Mike had hanging on a string over the sink.

'She's coming,' gasped Randy.

'Who's coming?'

'That woman.' I collapsed onto a chair, which in turn

nearly collapsed under me. 'You remember her—the one from the Arbuckle thing.'

'That—ah—' he gestured vaguely, Mike being a gentleman and not liking to use the expression *that red-hot smokin' piece of ass* out loud.

'She's . . .' I waved a hand. 'I don't know what she is. But she's on some kinda crazy mission. She blew up my place—and Randy's—and now . . .'

'She blew up your *houses*, are you kidding?'

'Yeah,' said Randy, real dry. 'We're kidding. Henry's been working on his costume for weeks.'

'Well, she ain't gonna find us in the Bayou,' said Mike robustly. 'Not unless she followed you, anyway. She follow you?'

'No, Mike, she didn't follow us,' said Randy. 'But she'll find us.' He mopped his face with his arm. 'She's got the—'

I stood up so fast the chair fell to pieces with the down-force.

'Don't say it,' I warned.

There was a knock at the door.

See, a cop knows something about the power of Voodoo—the power of belief. The Law's a funny thing. People believe in it, and they don't. In their heads, they know we're ordinary guys and gals, most us only educated to high school, a lot of us overweight and cynical and counting down to our twenty-five. They know we can't read minds or see through walls and the uniform ain't bullet-proof. They know Cop Glamour ain't the truth and we ain't Superman, but more often than not, when they hear that knock at the door, they *believe* it's true. And when that fear turns 'em weak at the knees—well, your job's half done afore you even get 'em down to the station.

I'm a law-abiding man; I was a cop for thirty-one years, I ain't never had the law come calling. That night was the only time I felt what it's like to be hiding and hoping and sweating with fear, hearing that knock at the door.

We peered outta the crack in the shutter. The lantern hanging on the porch was like a bonfire in the darkness.

'Good evening, gentlemen.' She stepped politely away from the door. 'I believe we have business to discuss. May I come in?'

There were smears of soot on her cheeks and that leather coat had taken some more damage. When she moved, she limped a little, and I thought I saw the sticky glisten of blood in her hair.

'May God, Jesus Christ and all the angels help us,' said Mike reverently.

'God won't help you, Officer Stone. The Supreme Being ceased His interest in man's affairs the moment His creation was complete. His son tried hard to save you from yourselves, but sometimes, only your own personal blood will atone. Have your friends explained?'

Keep her talking—make a connection . . . we all knew the drill.

'No, ma'am, we have not,' I managed. 'Perhaps you could—'

It was definitely blood in her hair—when she touched it, it smeared her fingers red. I wondered how bad she was hurt.

'You're lying, Henry. But I'll let that one go. So, let's recap, shall we?' She held up three fingers. The index finger was missing a nail. 'Mr Arbuckle. Mr Santiago. One more left to remember. Three men, dead by your hands. And I'm here to collect payment.'

'What is it you want?' Mike demanded.

She scratched impatiently at the sticky patch in her hair and swayed a little.

'I'd like to come inside, Office Stone.' She was battered and bleeding and I was fairly sure she'd taken a serious head injury, but her smile was still like an angel's. 'To talk about the time you shot Victor Jones.'

I don't know the name for the colour Mike went when he heard that name, but it wasn't nothing you'll see interior designers recommending.

'How does it feel to shoot an unarmed man in the back?'

'I don't know—'

'Yes you do, Officer Stone. You know exactly how that feels. Mr Jones wasn't threatening you, was he? He didn't respond to your instruction because he didn't *hear* it, did he? Can you remember why he didn't hear you?'

'Ma'am, he turned and left the room, contrary to my clear—' Another first—seeing that pleading expression on a cop.

'He was going to the *bedroom* where his *two year old daughter* was *screaming* for her daddy to come get her. She was screaming because Officer Lewis had just *climbed in through her window with a gun*, the gun he *shot her daddy with* when he came through the door, although he was already mortally wounded by your shot, wasn't he? Officer Lewis's shot was just the cherry on top, wasn't it?'

'I didn't—' Mike swallowed, tried again. 'I didn't mean—'

'I'm really not interested in motivations. I don't want to hear you apologise, or beg. I'm just the debt collector, and all I want is payment.' A trickle of red-black blood inched down her forehead. She wiped it away with a hand that had a blister the size of a tomato. 'So, for the record, are you going to let me in?'

'How do you know this?' Randy whispered. 'How do you know?'

'Because it's my job to know. Are you going to let me over the threshold?'

We looked at each other.

'Not while I still got a hole in my ass,' said Mike, who sometimes wasn't all that much of a gentleman underneath. 'I don't know who or what you are, but you ain't coming into my home at my invitation, and I bet you can't smash the shutters in quicker'n we can run. So, what you gonna do about it?'

She laughed.

'Not while you still got a hole in your ass,' she repeated. 'What an excellent phrase. I must remember it. Well, as you wish.'

Here it comes, I thought, and closed my eyes, waiting for the *ka-boom* that would take us all either up to heaven, or down into hell.

But it didn't come.

What happened next was that she kicked the door down, and stood there, panting, her hair all over her face.

We coulda taken her. Three of us, one of her, no-one to see. Her one possible advantage had been whether she could smash her way in faster'n we could get the door open, and she'd just thrown it away.

But we didn't. Her coat was half burned off of her, and she was covered with scratches and burns, and *still* she was beautiful. She looked like an avenging angel, which I guess mighta been what she was, and we cowered. Three grown men, and we cowered.

'I thought you couldn't come in if we didn't invite you!' Randy screamed. 'I thought that was the rules!'

'Ways and means, Officer Lewis.' She nodded to the fish over the sink. 'Death in the house allows many things access. Of course, now I'll die too; but that's fine.'

'We can work this out,' said Mike, doggedly sticking to the script. 'We can—'

'No, we can't,' I said.

Mike and Randy clearly thought I'd gone nuts.

'You've gone nuts,' said Mike.

'Nope,' I told him. 'She's right. We gotta pay for what we did. We killed, the three of us.'

'But we *had* to—'

'No, we didn't.' She nodded approvingly. 'I *did* shoot Ben Arbuckle because I was pissed off and too hot and I'd had enough. I thought he was Robaire Lebrun, but that don't make it right. We all chose the tune we danced to. Now we got to pay the piper.'

'Henry, I always knew you were the smart one,' she said. She was holding the last bomb in her hand, tossing it thoughtfully up and down, that blister quivering like jelly. 'You might be a fat middle-aged redneck, but that's okay by me. Anything else you want to say?'

'Yeah,' I said. 'I guess—I guess I'm sorry. I don't know if I'm sorry cuz I'm gonna die, or sorry cuz I finally see the evil of killing someone just because I could.' I looked right at her. 'Which is what you're doing now, ain't it? You're gonna kill all three of us, just because you can.'

'That's about the size of it,' she agreed. 'Officer Stone, Officer Lewis, anything you want to say before I end it all?'

'Can't we talk about—' started Randy.

'Just get on with it,' growled Mike.

She pulled the fuse.

❧

I thought I'd heard how loud an explosion could be that evening, but it turned out I hadn't. This was so loud it was almost silent, and it felt like it was happening right inside my head. I thought I'd feel my brains leaking outta my ears any second. And then I didn't have time to worry about my brains, cos my whole self was flying upwards, like it'll be when the Rapture comes, only I doubt getting Raptured up's gonna hurt quite so much, and also I don't think our Lord Jesus will set our clothes on fire. Up and up and up, and then down and down and down, bits of the shack falling around us like straw. And then the Bayou opened her cold arms and welcomed us into the mud and the slime, and I went from burning to drowning, and the mud leaked in through my nose, and I wondered if the gators'd mind me turning up on their doorsteps half-cooked.

And then—

Then someone was kissing me. A kiss that brought a dead man back to life, and I don't mean resuscitation. I've given *that* kiss myself, sometimes after scraping clots of blood or vomit out first, which ain't much fun. I could feel her hands on my face, the strength in them bringing me back to life, and she tasted like ripe peaches on a hot day.

I opened my eyes.

I was lying on the path near where Mike's hut used to be. The debris was burning merrily; I felt the warmth from fifteen feet away. The thunderstorm—*her* thunderstorm—had stopped. I was still wearing bits of my bathrobe and she was still just about covered with the tatters of that leather coat. Half her hair was burnt off and I could see the head wound she'd been scratting at earlier, a big hole in the skull, pink and white jello showing. Only took one look to see she was almost done.

And she'd spent the last of her strength dragging me outta that swamp.

'Why . . .' I coughed, tasted mud, threw up, tried again. I could only tell I was talking from the vibrations in my head. 'Why'd you save me? Is it because . . .' a bit more throwing up. She waited patiently. 'Is it because I repented?' She shook her head. 'Then why? Why me?' I looked around. 'It is just me, ain't it? You ain't got Mike and Randy stashed away somewhere too?'

'No.'

'Why me?' I repeated. 'You said you came for payment. Three of us for three of them. Wasn't that the deal?'

'You still don't know who I am or who sent me, do you?' I could hear her perfectly, even though the rest of the world had gone silent. Her eyes were liquid like the water she'd pulled me from, and just as hard to read. 'But how could you ever recognise me, you poor stupid white man? Your God let His own beloved son be slaughtered, and never took revenge. The word that moves me is the prayer of three mothers, whose love you spilled with the blood of their boy-children. They wept, and they prayed, and they called on the powerful female spirits, Marinette and Erzuli Dantor. They told their sorrows and they made their sacrifices, until finally they summoned me up out of the ground to give them justice. But even that old, wild Justice has a mercy your God will never understand. The love of a mother who prays for you nightly is a powerful and mysterious thing. Henry Reynolds, be grateful you still have a mother.'

And then, as God's my witness, she threw back her head and howled aloud to the sky. And when she ran away into the Bayou, well, you can think I was dazed, or confused, or just plumb crazy, but I'll tell you anyway, and you can laugh if you want, because I *know* what I saw.

As she took off into the night, she was just about the biggest damned she-wolf I ever saw.

Interview #15

—Cornelia Sahani Adair
Blue Ridge Mountains, Boone, North Carolina

S O YOU FOUND the studio. Well, young man, you passed the first test at least.

I hope my agent explained the conditions of this interview? And you're absolutely sure you're comfortable with that? All right, then. Take your clothes off behind that screen.

You did understand that condition, didn't you? You can interview me, if I can sculpt you. And I'm afraid I'm not interested in sculpting your clothes.

Sit on that stool, please. I'll be working in wax, it's not my usual choice, but something tells me this won't work if we're shouting over the sound of hammering. Don't look so scared, I promise not to bite you. If it's any consolation, I'm rather nervous myself. You only have to bare your body. You're asking *me* to bare my soul.

Do you know the most insulting compliment you can pay a woman? Tell her she's got beautiful hair.

My earliest memory: kindergarten, playing with plasticine, making a rabbit; a sudden cohort of little girls.

'Why are you so funny-looking?' their leader demanded.

When you're a child, your body's your home; not beautiful, not ugly, just *there*. I had no words.

The teacher arrived to rescue me.

'Cornelia is not funny-looking,' she said severely. 'We don't say that here. We're all different, in our own good ways. Everyone has something beautiful about them.' She looked at me, and faltered. I was tall and lumpy, incongruous green eyes beneath an epicanthic fold, skin neither fair nor bronze, but a dull mud colour, with a nose that worked on my father but not on a woman, never mind a little girl.

'Look,' she said, determined. 'Doesn't Cornelia have beautiful hair?'

With that sentence, she imprisoned me.

Turn this way a little, please—thank you.

A memory of my mother's shop; a cornucopia of woods and fabrics and gleaming metals, cushions and tables and mirrors with enormous frames and things to put in fireplaces instead of fires. It was like climbing into a jewellery box.

I was mostly terrified of breaking things. My body was a constant, unwelcome surprise; I grew fast and I was never sure how much of me there was at any one time. In a mirror, my face loomed out of the darkness. I staggered backwards, knocked something alabaster off something else gilded, then put a sticky hand down on a third thing all velvety, leaving a stain. My mother didn't scold, which made it worse—the implication, of course, being that I couldn't help it.

She taught me the love of beauty and the agony of its absence. I would have given anything to belong to her world. I walked in beauty, but I had no part of it. I could only look and yearn.

You don't like to hear me talking so candidly, do you? The word *ugly* distresses you. Like all attractive people, you think *ugly* is a four-letter word. But this is the first lesson every artist must learn: to see things as they truly are.

A memory of my father: weekends and vacations when I ceased to be the strange half-Indian girl in Sacramento, and became the strange half-white girl on the North Carolina Reservation. He taught me the things he thought I needed to know, which in practice meant the things *he* needed to know to survive on twenty-two thousand dollars a year and no health insurance. He had the skills of successful poverty: repairing machines, chopping wood, building fires, mending clothes, fixing houses, cleaning guns, hunting meat, cleaning and cooking it afterwards. I don't think that was particularly because he was Native American. It's just what blue-collar fathers from North Carolina do. He taught me to fix cars, since that was his trade, to weld, to change a plug, to use power tools; the kind of things he'd have taught his son if he'd had one, but I was what there was, so, like my mother, he made do.

The memory of the day he first took me hunting. The stars watched us as we left and the air was clammy. He'd been teaching me to shoot—a skill to be acquired with respect, with slowness. For the white people it wasn't deer-hunting season, but a Cherokee Indian on his own tribal land doesn't worry too much about the rules of white people. By a still forest pool, he tested the wind, and led me through mud and green moss to the far side of the water.

A white-tail buck breasted the thin grey light. His head

dipped, raised, dipped again. The wind blew his scent to me and I inhaled it deeply.

He was perfect, in his prime, glossy and well-fed, his antlers soft with velvet, his dappled coat smooth and without flaw. He was beautiful, but we were hungry.

I took careful aim at the heart. I saw the leap and the drop and the twitch and the stillness.

By myself, I cleaned him and bled him and thanked the earth for her bounty. My father nodded approvingly. I hoisted him across my shoulders and carried him to the truck. We let him hang for a week, then butchered him, froze him and roasted a haunch, which we ate sitting by a fire I'd chopped the wood for.

This is another lesson all artists need to learn, including you. Beauty is beauty, but it doesn't fill your belly. If you want to eat, sometimes you have to compromise.

We got on all right, my father and I. He didn't talk much, but fathers often don't. At first I thought he was keeping his thoughts to himself. Later I realised he simply didn't think all that much. His life was hard and rough and left little room for introspection.

Was I happier with my father? I suppose I was less *unhappy*, less conscious of what a misfit I was. I do better in big, empty spaces, and there were plenty of those where he lived. He didn't have much of anything, so there was less for me to break, and I was handier with a wood-axe and a rifle than a paintbrush or a needle. Five foot twelve and built like a linebacker makes you good at outdoor living . . . it's time we took a break; you'll get cramp if you sit still much longer.

You're sure you don't mind if we keep going? You're

right, of course; I don't feel comfortable if I'm not working. I've become very self-indulgent.

Turn your head away, please.

Okay. A memory from college; a hot April night, Sophomore year, two days before my twentieth birthday. I was determined not to begin my third decade as a virgin.

I applied make-up, bought that afternoon. I put on underwear that pushed me upwards and inwards. I put on a scarlet silk dress a theatre major called Janice had made for me. I unbraided my hair and brushed it smooth and straight. I forced on high heels that were slightly too small. I limped downtown to a bar I had heard Janice mention.

I ordered a beer and felt strangely at home. Men looked at me and did not look away. A man sat down beside me and we talked a little. He told me his name was Rolando. He wanted to be an actor.

In the motel room, he closed the door behind us. He was even more nervous than I, which I found charming. He was clumsy, but so was I; he was shorter than me, even without the heels, but most men were. He was good-looking and gentle, which was enough for the first time, I thought. I had to kiss him first. He tasted of beer and peppermint.

I could feel his eagerness, which I found unexpectedly thrilling. I helped him help me out of my dress. Then he stopped.

'Jesus,' he gasped.

Something was wrong, but I couldn't see what. His hands flinched away as if I was a hot skillet.

'But you're—' His face was horrified.

I looked at him blankly.

'Sweet Jesus, I'm sorry,' he said, and he really sounded sorry. 'I thought . . .'

'What?' I asked.

'I thought you . . .' He hesitated. 'I thought you were a man.'

I've often been told that white people find my face difficult to read. For this one poor, thin mercy, I was profoundly grateful.

'But I'm wearing a dress,' I said. 'I'm wearing make-up. I'm wearing high heels. I have long hair.'

'I'm sorry,' he repeated. 'You just — you're so — um — tall.' Beneath his skin I could see the blood rising. The word *ugly* perched on his tongue. 'I — I'm not gay, I just — wanted —' Maybe I looked inscrutable, but his face was easy to read; he was beginning to pity me. 'Didn't you know what kind of bar it was?'

'I just heard a friend mention it once,' I said. 'I think I'll go now.'

I'd like to say I can laugh about it, but the fact is that I can't. It was the single most humiliating experience of my life.

A memory of my first and only job interview, a week after graduation. The Blue Ridge Mountains are surprisingly rich in places selling beautiful things.

My future boss was in her late thirties, black hair in fierce ringlets around her heart-shaped face, and enormous black eyes that drilled into you and made you squirm. She wore a lot of black, which suited her. Her gallery was a cool, quiet space with high ceilings, which suited me. I could move freely among the lovely objects without fear of smudging or chipping or destroying.

'You've no experience,' said Amaranth.

I could have said, *You're not paying enough for experience.* I could have said, *You knew that before you said you'd see me.*

I could have said, *Everyone has to start somewhere.* I could have said, *I'm willing to learn.*

'I'm sorry,' I said.

'You're very tall, aren't you?'

There was nothing to say about that, so I kept silent.

'Your hair is lovely.'

'Thank you.'

'And your degree's in . . . ?'

'Liberal arts, majoring in art history. I graduated from Appalachian State.'

'I was thinking of a man,' she mused. 'I have a sculptor at the moment . . .' She looked me up and down. 'How strong are you?'

A granite bear, three feet tall, snarled from a plinth. I put my arms around it, bent my knees, tested the weight and awkwardness. A brief effort and I had it securely, first against my chest, then high in the air. I heard Amaranth inhale sharply.

'That's a three-thousand dollar—' she let her breath out again as I lowered the bear back onto the plinth. 'Okay, you're strong enough.' She looked at me narrowly. 'What do you think of it?'

I looked at the bear.

'I think it's very ugly,' I said. 'But I can't afford it anyway.'

Amaranth laughed.

'What would you buy? If you had the money?'

In the window was a semi-abstract oil painting: thick, exuberant brush-strokes in greens, blues, browns, ambers, silvers, golds. It was like looking at the soul of the mountain. It lit up the street, calling customers inside. I hadn't dared look for the price ticket. She saw me glance.

'The Blue Ryan,' she said, purring and possessive. 'You

have good taste.' She looked at me thoughtfully. 'I can't pay much—'

'I don't need much,' I said hastily. It was true; I'd learned to live frugally.

'All right then, Cornelia,' she said, smiling. 'You can start Monday.'

A memory from a cool spring evening, eighteen months after I started. Amaranth didn't like her hulking half-Indian girl lurching out from behind things at the customers. She encouraged me to spend time in back instead. But when the customers went home, I'd sweep the floor and dream over the beauty dripping off the walls.

In her office, Amaranth was on the phone. I lingered.

'Blue,' she said, her voice loving. 'Don't be silly. Of course you'll—'

A pause.

'You need quiet. In the mountains, it'll come.'

Another pause.

'The studio's yours as long as you need it. I'll drive you up myself. And, darling . . .'

Amaranth had a habit of sleeping with the artists whose work she sold; it helped ensure their loyalty and keep her percentages high. But Blue was the first I'd heard her call darling. Of course, he was by far the most talented, and also the most saleable, despite the dizzying prices she put on his work. Everything he sent sold within weeks—everything except that one piece, *Ancestral*, that hung in the window. I'd noticed we'd received nothing new from him in months.

I sometimes got to work half an hour early so I could spend time looking at that painting.

Okay, stop, stop, stop. Don't tell me you're all right;

you're cold and you're cramped. Stand up. Don't be ridiculous, I've seen it already. Stretch your legs. Now your arms. Flex your toes. And your fingers. Better? Good. There's a blanket behind the screen. Wrap up and I'll make coffee.

Don't look so panicked. I've started this interview and I'll certainly finish it. And don't apologise, either. Artists can become the most hideous monsters if we're not kept in check. We become obsessed with our work, convinced it matters so much to get every detail right, forgetting there's a world out there that got along fine all this time without our shapes, our colours, our textures. We shut ourselves away in our high towers and think we've found sanctuary. But there's a fine line between *sanctuary* and *prison*.

The memory of the first time I saw him.

I drove my father's old Hilux as high as I could, then hiked the rest, following a map I'd furtively scribbled in Amaranth's office. My goal was an X called Studio, three miles from the truck. Inside my clothes I was warm; outside my clothes, my face and hands tasted the coming winter. I was almost certainly one of only two people within a twenty-mile radius.

Nobody answered when I knocked, but I went in anyway. The door opened onto the living room. To the left was a lean-to kitchen, the sink piled high with plates, and a bathroom with the smell of damp coiling out. Two more doors—one to the right, one on the back wall—were closed. On the table, a sandwich lay curling and dead beside a mug of water. By the sofa, a mound of blankets looked like a shucked snakeskin. The huge wood stove was unlit. It was very cold.

I heard a man's voice, his accent softly Irish. He sounded on the verge of panic.

'Amaranth, I'm sorry, okay? I'll be ready for the Holiday exhibition, I just—'

'It's not Amaranth,' I said.

There was a pause, then the door on the back wall opened and a man stood there. He was the same height as me. He had grey eyes and clear white skin. His brown hair curled wildly around his head and spilled onto his shoulders in Cavalier ringlets.

He was beautiful.

'Oh,' he said. He looked terrified.

'Hello,' I said gently.

'Who are you?'

'My name's Cornelia.' I found I was irritated by the way he was staring at me. 'I work for Amaranth. She's gone to Goose Creek on business. I came to see if you're all right.'

'That means she's gone to see Simeon Nadiki,' he said savagely. 'Is she sleeping with him, do you think?'

I knew she was, but didn't see why I should tell him.

'How on earth would I know?'

'You work for her—'

'That doesn't mean I know who she's fucking in her spare time.' I stopped myself from putting my hand to my mouth; I'd never said the word *fucking* out loud in my life before.

He was still staring at me.

'Have you always been so tall?'

'No,' I said. 'I was slightly shorter the day I was born. Have you always been so rude?'

'No,' he said instantly. 'I was slightly more civilised before I committed to a major new exhibition by Christmas. Sorry. I haven't spoken to anyone but Amaranth for—' He looked around helplessly. 'I'm sorry it's so cold. I can't get the fire to stay lit, I can't get the cooker to work. It wasn't so bad in the summer, but—'

I looked around. He was ravishing, but clueless; left to himself, it was more than possible he'd either freeze or starve before the spring came.

'What does Amaranth eat?'

'She brings food with her,' he said, looking vague. 'Smoked salmon, brie, champagne—you know the stuff she likes. I don't mind, I'm not interested in food, I just wish I could—' He thumped the doorframe in frustration. 'If I could just *work*! You can't *imagine*—'

Through the doorway was a huge white space.

'Can I see?' I asked.

'No you bloody well can't.'

'Fine. Then I'll leave you to it.' He glared at me defiantly. 'I wanted to make sure you're all right. I've done that. Now I'm going.'

'Okay.' He looked humble. 'I'll make you a sandwich first if you like.'

It was the way he caved in so completely that changed my mind. Beauty generally excuses its possessors from learning humility. The unexpected combination was disarming.

Are you hungry, by the way?

Of course it's good; I made it myself. Home-made bread is always better. It makes me laugh when people talk about the *slow food revolution*. We're just rediscovering what our ancestors always knew. But that's the job of every generation; to re-invent what our parents told us, and imagine ourselves pioneers.

The rest of that afternoon. The first thing I did was get the fire going. He'd tried, but he clearly didn't have the faintest idea; he'd just piled logs onto screws of newsprint and put a match to it. The bread was stale, but there was flour and butter and yeast in the pantry, so I mixed and kneaded and left the dough to prove while I split logs, my braid falling over my shoulder with every swing of the axe. I checked the gas cylinder and found, as I'd expected, that it was full but not connected properly, got the stove working, then put the bread in the oven. I went through the ancient freezer and found a few pounds of dubious ground beef, something shrivelled and pale that could have been a chicken portion, and a lot of frost. Whenever I looked up, he was watching me. I was unused to being observed, and glared at him. He didn't seem to mind.

'Were you actually planning on surviving this winter?' I asked as we ate warm bread and canned soup at the table. He'd shed layers as the room warmed up; I could see now he was far too thin for his height.

There's tinned stuff in the larder. I don't mind cold food. Besides, if I can't paint, it doesn't matter.' I looked at him incredulously. 'Okay, to you that sounds ridiculous. But if I can't deliver what I promised . . .'

I found him absurd, but he was so guileless that it was hard to mock him openly.

'Amaranth made me, you see. There are thousands of artists, most better than me. But she chose me. And she's so beautiful. God, she's beautiful . . .'

And she gets her pound of flesh, I thought, looking at the fine bones of his hand and wrist. *There's hardly a picking left on you.*

Memories of that winter.

Hiking up the trail through crisp frost, plants crunching beneath my boots. I had four rabbits slung around my neck—a bit thin and stringy, but left to hang and stewed slowly, they'd be all right. I'd fixed a wire cage against the cabin wall so they could hang in peace.

Blue was at the table, feverishly scribbling with a thick pencil. He covered the sketch with another sheet when I came in. There had been no dirty plates since I showed him how the water-heater worked and explained to him I was nobody's unpaid skivvy.

His smile was lovely. He'd gained a little weight, which he'd badly needed. He looked tired, but purposeful.

The door to the bedroom was ajar and I could see the huge, wrought-iron bed that almost filled it. The blankets on the sofa, where he usually slept, were folded where I'd left them.

Of course, I knew she visited him. In fact, I made a point of listening in to her phone calls to make sure we wouldn't meet. I wasn't jealous, how could I be? The idea of rivalry was absurd. But still, I shut that door as soon as I got the opportunity.

Another day, another memory: making pastry. It was hard work—I'd forgotten to take the butter out of the pantry, and the rubbing-in made my hands ache. My hair was full of static electricity and strands escaped my braid and hung about my face. When I pushed them away, I got pastry in my hair.

I laid a pale pastry lid over fragrant stew and crimped the edge, then used the trimmings to make a running rabbit for decoration.

'That's pretty,' said Blue, glancing over. He was beside me making bread. I'd insisted he learn the basics at least, and he'd been surprisingly happy to learn. I felt his breath against my cheek.

'I'll give it to Amaranth,' I said. 'She'll sell it for nine hundred dollars, plus sales tax.'

'Is that what she sells my stuff for?' he asked.

I snorted.

'Hardly.'

'Not that much? Oh, well. Maybe one day.' He was trying to be casual, but it didn't quite come off. I was surprised.

'You do know how much she charges, right?'

He shrugged.

'I've never really bothered. As long as people are buying.'

I thought about the painting in the window. She could have sold it dozens of times over, but she insisted it wasn't for sale. The last customer to enquire had offered forty thousand dollars.

Making sure Blue Ryan didn't freeze, starve or burn to death was taking up enough of my time as it was. I couldn't be responsible for his self-esteem into the bargain.

'Better to sell ten things for a dollar than nothing for ten,' I told him instead. 'That dough's ready.'

'How can you tell?'

'It goes silky. Feel.'

Together, we caressed the dough. The feel of his skin against mine made me cross. Our hands looked alike, broad and muscled, but mine was rougher, the skin darker, the nails ragged, the skin scratched where I'd scrubbed impatiently with a stiff wire brush to get dried dirt out from the cracks.

A walk through the woods, me leading, Blue following. He was the most inept woodsman I'd ever seen, tripping on everything except the things he crashed into. When we reached the top of the ridge, he was sweating.

'Have you ever actually left the cabin?' I asked him. 'How can you paint a mountain you never see?'

'I do go out,' he said, then grinned. 'Just, you know, not very successfully. I sprained my ankle last summer putting my foot down a rabbit hole. Took hours to get back. But I remember everything I see.'

Side by side, we looked at the view. I picked twigs and leaves out of my braid. From the corner of my eye I could see his long, lean thighs encased in denim. I tried hard not to look.

'Why do you sleep on the sofa?' I asked him suddenly.

To my surprise, he blushed, that pale Irish skin turning crimson. When he raised a hand to hide it, even his palms were red.

'Me and Amaranth—' he was stammering. 'She's shared that bed—you know, with—there was a guy before me—she had a forge put in for him, he must have been special—and before that was a girl, a sculptor—'

A girl? This was a part of Amaranth I hadn't seen. His hands were trembling. I wanted to ask, *Do you mind that she sleeps with other people?* I wanted to ask, *Have you slept with anyone else?* I wanted to ask, *Why do you let her treat you that way?* It was like picking a scab; it hurts, but you can't not do it.

'How did you meet her?' I demanded.

'I was at college in Dublin. We had to paint something from our childhoods. Well, my mammy had this vegetable garden, grew a special kind of lettuce she was crazy about. She said she almost lived off it when she was expecting me. I did a study of it, called *Salad*. I look back at it now . . . but I was pleased at the time. It got into the exhibition. Amaranth saw it, and . . .' he shrugged. 'My mam wasn't pleased, I was only nineteen. But my da said they had to let me go.'

'And are you — are you in love with her?'

'Am I — oh, God Almighty . . .' He turned away from me. '*Don't* ask me that, okay? Please, Cornelia, just — don't.'

'Okay,' I said. I couldn't think of anything else to say.

The memory of the day it happened.

The cabin was empty when I arrived. Blue's boots and jacket were missing. I remembered the rabbit hole and the sprained ankle and hoped he hadn't been gone too long. If he was lost, he'd be easy enough to track. The day we'd climbed the ridge, he'd left a trail like a blindfolded Minotaur.

The door to the studio was ajar. I hesitated for about a quarter of a second.

The studio was the entire other half of the cabin, one huge white-painted room with a glass roof. Canvases stood with their faces to the wall. An easel in the centre was covered with a sheet. A stool, at the wrong height to be comfortable if it was upright, lay on its side on the floor. A small table, also the wrong height, spilled paints and brushes onto the floor.

But I was distracted by the coke-burning forge that squatted on a deep brick hearth, ugly and functional, its wide mouth hungry. An oxy-acetylene torch leaned against its blackened side. An anvil and vice were built into the floor, surrounded with slate tiles. A cloth bag held a collection of tools.

I looked at the forge. The forge looked back.

I slung the coke hod over my shoulder and went to the shed. I filled it and went back inside, flinging my dusty braid out of the way. I built the fire and fed it patiently. The heat scorched my face.

Back in the shed, I found riches undreamed of. Long,

straight poles that begged to be curved and coiled, scraps and oddments with forms half-visible, awaiting someone with the strength and vision to wrest them out, flat sheets that could be beaten and shaped into—into—

I didn't even realise I was running until I got back inside and found I was panting. It didn't occur to me to put on gloves, I was in too much of a hurry, but I found a pair of goggles and jammed them on.

The lessons of my father and my mother; the ordered direction of physical effort, and the making of beauty.

The next few hours are something of a blur.

May I touch your hands? I want to feel the shape of them.

You're absolutely sure? Thank you.

This memory is filled with the scent of burning hair. It was the torch that did it; I'd forgotten how careful you have to be. My braid strayed into its path; there was a bright flare and the smell of burning keratin. I slapped it hastily out and swore under my breath.

From just behind me, Blue said, 'Cornelia, what are you doing?'

I turned around and nearly took him out with the torch; he jumped backwards just in time.

'What does it look like?' I demanded, feeling as if he'd caught me in my bath.

'No,' he said, very gently. He took the torch from me and laid it on the floor before I could kill him with it. 'I mean, what are you *doing*? Why are you coming up here, baking bread, chopping wood, cooking, washing up—keeping an idiot like me alive—when you could be doing—*this*?'

We looked at the object taking shape beneath my hands. It was a chair with a table attached, built for an artist—for the artist who, I'd noticed months before, was exactly the same height as me. The heavy base would keep the seat steady, unlike the stool which fell over as soon as he forgot himself and moved. Sinuous coils of iron made a stable but flexible pillar, something to absorb his restless energy. The seat curved down at the front and up at the back, so he could lean forward to paint and backwards to examine. The table, also mounted on iron coils, and on the left because he was, like me, left-handed, had a lip all around to stop things rolling off. I'd cut a hole where a cup would later stand to keep brushes in. I planned to make some removable ridged trays, so the paints could lie without confusion, and picked up without needing to scrabble. But first I had formed a leaping rabbit from scraps and bits and fragments, a touch of whimsy to remind me of the day we made bread and rabbit pie in the chilly kitchen, and I was welding it to the back of the chair when Blue came in and caught me.

'What are you talking about?' I asked. I craved one of the white sheets to cover my work.

'This is what you should be doing for real, it's incredible—'

'Don't touch it!' I yelled, too late. He winced and put his fingers in his mouth.

'Idiot,' I said.

'Says the woman who was setting fire to her hair when I came in.'

I inspected the end of my braid. It was half a foot shorter, fused and crisp.

'Why do you have it so long anyway?' he asked.

'Because—'

I couldn't bring myself to say it. He knew me as a brisk, efficient workhorse, sexless as a fencepost. I didn't want him to see that, inside my head, I was also a woman.

'It annoys you *all the time*,' he said. 'It gets in your way when you do anything. I'm amazed you haven't taken it off with the wood-axe before now.'

I couldn't think of anything to say that wouldn't sound absurd. I glared at him instead, but it didn't seem to work.

'Why don't you let me cut it for you?' he asked. 'Cornelia, will you let me cut your hair?'

With your permission, I'm going to touch your head and face now.

Close your eyes, please.

He tied a black ribbon around the top of my braid, at the base of my skull. Just—there. I thought about the hours of work, combing and conditioning and waiting for it to dry. I felt the weight fall away as the scissors sheared through.

'There,' he said.

I turned my head experimentally. It felt light and free. He was still standing behind me. With my hair gone, I could feel the warmth of his body. He felt very close. He did not move away.

'Shorter,' I said.

He hesitated, then his hands lightly brushed my head. 'Okay.'

He began to lift and snip, lift and snip. I thought of sheep-shearing, the ewe pressed against the man's crotch, the arms wrapped round, the clippers moving over her body, the sheep springing free.

'It's coming out kind of spiky,' he warned after a while.

'I don't care,' I said. I could only find short, snappy sentences; I had no breath for more. His fingers touched my ear.

'How's that?' he said. His voice was blurred, as if he was tired, or drunk.

I ran my fingers over my head. It felt like thistledown.

'Shorter,' I repeated.

He came back with an electric shaver, which normally lived a precarious existence on the shelf above the bath. The vibrations travelled over my scalp and down through my chest. I tried to remember when anyone had last touched me as intimately as Blue was touching me now, and came up empty and yearning.

'It's finished,' he said at last. 'It's all gone. All but the last few millimetres.' His voice still had that thick, blurred quality. I thought of the taste of wine.

I ran my hands over my naked scalp. It felt like suede. My head was so light I thought it might float off my shoulders.

'That feels strange,' I mumbled. 'But kind of good.'

Behind me, Blue groaned out loud.

I stroked my head, amazed at the shape of my own skull.

'Do you want to feel?'

'Cornelia . . . for God's sweet sake . . .' He sounded furious.

I could still feel the vibration of his touch all over my body.

'What's wrong?' I asked.

'What's *wrong*? How can you sit there and ask me what's wrong? Ah, God, Cornelia, you *must* know how I—as if I haven't dreamed about—'

Then his hands were on my scalp, caressing, stroking, and I realised that they were shaking.

Afterwards, we lay on the floor in each other's arms and watched the sky turn black through the glass roof.

Actually, I think . . . I'll have to skip a little.

Why? How can I put this?

There are parts of your body you won't let me touch, aren't there? Even though you know I've seen them. Sight and touch are very different senses.

Well, there are parts of my soul I can't let you put your hands on either.

But I'll tell you four things I don't remember, because they never happened. And it didn't occur to me to want them. What we had was more than enough, more than I'd dreamed.

He didn't paint anything.

I didn't make anything.

He never told me I was beautiful.

And he never said he loved me.

The memory of the day it ended.

I parked in the usual spot and hiked through snow. I wore woollen long johns under men's jeans, a checked shirt covered with a jumper and a peacoat, and a shapeless hat given to me years ago by my father. My naked head was still unused to the cold. In my rucksack I had venison steaks wrapped in paper.

In the studio, the forge was lit, he always kept it lit for us, and the reflection of the firelight flickered in the glass ceiling. Someone sat in the chair I'd made, but it wasn't Blue. I only struggled to recognise her because she was out of context, and naked into the bargain. Actually, she had far more right to be there than I.

'Hello,' said Amaranth.

I thought she had a dead animal on her lap, but it

turned out to be the long braid of my discarded hair, tied top and bottom with black ribbon.

'Well, you certainly took care of him, didn't you?' said Amaranth. 'Don't worry. I'm not jealous. Blue's just a man after all, they take it where they can find it.' She laughed. 'You didn't have to leave your job over this, you know. And especially not by letter. *Family circumstances call me away*, indeed. That was rude, Cornelia. But you've always been a rude, uncouth girl. Listening at doors. Taking things that don't belong to you.'

I could have said, *How did you find out?* I could have said, *I thought you weren't jealous.* I could have said, *Blue isn't a thing, he's a person.* I could have said, *You left him here without even bothering to check he was warm.* I could have said, *He chose me.* I could have said any of those things.

I looked at her, slender and lithe and beautiful, and said nothing.

'I suppose I should thank you for keeping him alive,' said Amaranth, stroking that braid of black hair. 'But he doesn't need you any more. He didn't want to tell you himself, but he's had enough of you now. Sex with you was just part of the creative process, like a pregnant woman eating coal. He's finished the work he promised, and he's coming back to civilisation. And you . . .' she laughed. 'You can go and deal with those *family circumstances* of yours.'

You can use silence like a shield, or like a sword. It was the only weapon I had.

'Did you make this chair?' she asked disdainfully. 'It's far too high to be comfortable. And it tilts forward.'

I could have said, *I didn't make it for you.*

Amaranth stood up. The braid of hair fell to the floor as she showed me her beautiful witch's body in the firelight.

She looked at my clothes, at my hat clutched in my hand, at my shorn head.

'I hope you didn't imagine he was in love with you,' she said lightly, and laughed. 'Good God, look at you . . . how could he be?'

What came next? What can I say? I left the cabin, leaving my heart behind.

Time passed.

The memory of realising that actually, my life hadn't ended, that I still had something worth keeping. Blue had left me without even saying goodbye, but before he went, he'd shown me who I was. I found a job at a garage, a room in the owner's house, and space to build my own forge.

The first thing I made was frames for two sheets of mirror from a building supply yard. I mounted them on opposite walls of my room, so I could shave my head without having to guess and fumble.

After a year, I began to find purchasers for the things I made. After some more years, I had enough to leave the garage and rent a studio. Some more years, and my name was beginning to be known, and the things were called *pieces* and the prices went up. My life, my real life, began.

I found happiness.

The day I went to New York.

It's not a city I'm fond of, but a gallery had purchased one of my things—my *pieces*—and my agent insisted. I don't know why I'm being so coy; actually it was MOMA, and I went to gaze incredulously at the Cornelia Adair *Artist's Chair*, which I'd made nineteen of altogether, all commissions. This particular chair was for Jane Broadman, and when she died, they bought it from her daughter. Next, I was paraded around lesser but still prestigious galleries, which sold rather than collected, and finally driven to an alarmingly gracious home near Central Park where a man wanted me to make him a bathtub. Yes, really, that's what he wanted; a custom-made bathtub. Well, why not?

He saw me, and turned pale.

'But you're *her*,' he said.

I was baffled.

'You're the woman in the paintings.' He wore his clothes the way a tortoise wears its shell. 'Come with me.'

I decided the advantages of six inches, twenty pounds and thirty years would guard my honour. He unlocked two doors before we reached the room he wanted.

'This is my treasure-room,' he told me. I nodded, and tried not to laugh.

Then I was inside, and glad, as I've so often been, for the face my father gave me, the expression called *inscrutable*.

The woman in the pictures wasn't beautiful; he'd never said that, and she never had been. But she was the right size and shape for the life he showed. There she was carrying a stack of logs. I'd been warm from chopping them, so I'd hung my coat up. Turning away, I snagged my sweater on the nail. In the picture, the thread hung from my left elbow.

There I was scrubbing the dining table. My face was towards the viewer and my expression was threatening. That was the day I told him if he wanted every mouse on the mountain to live with him, that was his business, but I wasn't eating off a table with mouldy crumbs in the cracks, so he could clean it himself, or eat outside. I smiled at the memory.

There were my hands, large and muscled and square.

They were peeling a potato. There was a scratch on the back where I'd snagged it on a bramble, and my thumbnail was broken. How had he seen so much, so clearly? He'd only watched me for a few seconds before I gave him the carrots to scrape.

'I've bought one every year for the last fifteen years,' said the man.

Fifteen years? I added up quickly in my head.

Yes. Yes. Fifteen years.

'Every year, there's one of these,' said the man. 'Just one of this woman.' He glanced at me slyly. 'Of you.'

I saw my half-shaved head, and Blue's hand on my neck. The next was a nude, I didn't want to look at it with this strange chelonian man beside me.

'Why did you leave him?' he demanded.

I could have said, *That's none of your business.* I could have said, *I didn't realise how he felt.* I could have said, *He left me.*

He waited greedily.

'Why don't you show me where you want the bathtub?' I said.

The art world is small, and now I was looking instead of avoiding, it was easy to find him. His work in maturity fulfilled every promise: rich, deep, bruisingly beautiful. And every year, without fail, a study of me — a love letter shared with the world, a declaration, a plea. A message in a bottle. A howl to the moon.

I could have gone to him. I could have said, *I didn't know.* I could have said, *I'll never leave you.* I could have said, *I'm yours.* I could have said, *No-one else, ever, nor ever will . . .*

But I didn't do any of those things.

∽

My dear, you're so young, so romantic. You'll learn one day that love can be terribly destructive.

I lived in peace. Blue and Amaranth between them had broken my heart; but for anyone a little late in finding their true purpose, the heart is a troublesome organ, best left behind and forgotten.

And yet, when love passes . . .

I waited five more years.

What was I waiting for? Why, for it to *end*. I waited until, twenty-one years after that day on the mountain, there was no picture of me in his collection.

When I saw that, I went to see him. He wasn't so far away after all, just the other side of the Blue Ridge Mountains, in South Carolina.

There was grey in his hair, but he was still beautiful.

'You stopped painting me,' I said, over the coffee he made and the muffins I'd brought.

'It was time. Twenty years is long enough to break your heart over someone who doesn't love you back.'

'I worked that out the first year,' I told him.

He smiled.

'You were always cleverer than me. And tougher.'

'Ugly women have to be,' I said.

He took my rough, scarred hand and examined it closely.

'I knew you'd be amazing,' he said. 'These hands were never meant just for making bread.'

'Don't be ridiculous. Domestic skills keep food on the table while the artists shut themselves away and dream.'

He let my hand go again.

'Why did you leave?' he asked. 'What did I do wrong?'

'What are you talking about?'

'That note you left. *Family circumstances call me away. Cornelia.* Just that note, and you never came back.'

'But that was for Amaranth,' I said. 'I quit my job. *You* left *me*. I came to the cabin and she was waiting. She said you'd had enough of me. She said I was—' it was hard to speak. '—like coal for a pregnant woman. Just something you needed to help you create.'

'But that's what happened to me, too,' he said, confused. 'I went out for a walk. When I got back Amaranth was there. She said you'd had enough of me. Well, I could understand that. I said you wouldn't go without telling me, and she showed me the note.'

'And you believed that?'

'Well, why not?' he demanded with spirit. 'You bloody did.'

'But—'

I wanted to say, *that's different*. But he was right, it was exactly the same. I'd been distracted by the surface of things. I'd confused *beauty* with *rightness*.

'So why come now?' he asked me. 'All those years I'd have given anything, done anything, gone anywhere you wanted . . . and now—'

'Now it's gone,' I said.

'Yes,' he said wearily. 'Now it's gone.'

'Good,' I said.

'What the hell are you talking about?'

'If we'd stayed together, what do you think we'd have achieved? Would you have done—all this? Would I?' I waved at the half-finished works leaning on the walls. 'Love's a distraction. It takes too much time and effort.' He was so angry his fingers twitched. 'I know you don't want to hear this, Blue, but you remember how it was. We didn't do anything, *anything* but screw each other's

74

brains out on the studio floor. You couldn't work. Neither could I. We hardly ate, we couldn't even get dressed. We'd have killed each other in six months. People aren't meant to live that way.'

'Maybe I wanted to live that way!'

'Well, I didn't. I'd just found out who I really was. I wanted to go off and be myself for a while.'

'For *twenty years*?'

'Why not? I spent twenty years before that not having a clue. But now I'm ready for the next thing.'

'What *next thing*? It's gone, Cornelia, we wasted it all. *You* wasted it all. If you'd come to me even just last year . . . God, if you knew how I longed for you—the dreams I had about you, night after night—and now—'

'Now we can try again,' I said. 'Now, we can stand alone, not needing anybody. We can do whatever we want. We can be together, or not. We're strong enough to withstand each other.'

'What the hell are you playing at?' he demanded furiously. 'What makes you think you can do this? How can you just wander into my life and expect me to let you in? How fucking *dare* you?'

Twenty years ago he'd been so gentle, so humble, so grateful. It was refreshing to see him angry enough to want to hit me.

I kissed him.

Twenty years ago, it had been a wild journey across a storm-tossed sea. Now, we were arriving in safe harbour after a perilous and lonely voyage; we were returning to a place well-loved, seeing it with new eyes.

We were home.

And that's it, young man; you have my memories, the

most important memories of my life. Thank you for sharing yourself with me in return.

You'd like to see? Of course.

I'm glad you think it's beautiful; but I'd prefer you to say it will be *useful*. Something tells me your room back home is a mess, and that you lose your keys and your wallet and your tape recorder and your pens and your small change on a regular basis, and you can never find a piece of paper when you need one. When you go home to write this up . . . I thought this might help.

This is called the lost wax technique, by the way. In the process, the wax of the original form is lost; but what's left instead is equally beautiful, and far more durable.

And now you want to know why I wanted to touch your head and your hands, don't you? Well, I could tell you the answer, but I won't. Apart from anything else, my husband will be back soon.

You look very young, my dear, when you blush like that.

Interview #17

— 'Tom'
Skid Row, Los Angeles, CA

A H, T A K E A hike, you nosey son-of-a-bitch. I told
you last time. I don't give a good god-damn about
your project, and I *certainly* ain't tellin' you how I got
here. You think there's anything worthwhile down here
in the gutter? I'm telling you, boy; ain't *nothing* here but
horror and confusion and lost, desperate souls. Take your
lousy college project and your fucking liberal compassion
and your *I just rilly feel like there's a story to be told here,
sir,* bleeding-heart West-Coast bullshit and get the hell
outta here.

You, *again*? Got some *cojones* on you, aintcha? No offence.
And don't think I don't know why you're comin' after me
so desperate and hopeful-like; I know what they told you.
*Talk to Tom, he's got a vocabulary of thirty-eight thousand words,
even if half of them are fuckin' obscenities. He chose to be here, he
coulda been anything if'n he'd wanted. Tom, he's doing penance.*
You're only here because you reckon I'm more like you
than I am like them. You want to hear how a man starts
out cradled in his momma's arms and ends up rotting away
down here? Go talk to Ron, under the bridge. Charming
fella if you happen to catch him in the right phase of the
moon. Paranoid schizophrenic, self-medicates with booze.

Half the time he's shouting at the sky, the other half he's layin' in the mud . . . now *there's* a fascinating fucking journey for you; it's got everything. Tragedy. Pathos. Unexpected bouts of extreme violence.

Yeah, I had you pegged for a god-damn pussy the first time I laid eyes on you.

What is it this time . . . ? Oh, now you're gonna try and *buy* me off, huh. Well, I ain't for sale, and neither's my life story . . . what did you bring?

Glenfiddich Ten-Year-Old Single Malt, are you shittin' me? You bought a bottle of well-aged Scotch whisky to a down-and-out bum living on Skid Row?

Ah, knock that off, would ya? I ain't *dying*, you loser, I'm *laughing*. You finally managed to do something entertaining. And civilised. I hope you brought glasses. You can't drink *this* stuff outta the bottle.

You *did* bring glasses. Huh . . .

Well, okay. I'll make a deal with you. I ain't gonna tell you *my* story. My story's my business, and that ain't for sale. But I'll tell you a fable of the streets; a true morality tale for our times; a story every wet-behind-the-ears starry-eyed idiot oughta hear at least once. This is the story of a man who managed to get himself a ticket for the Money Train. This story is about a man called Jack.

Jack English was a farmer-boy, grew up in Idaho. Classic smallholding, the kind there ain't really room for no more in this fine and copasetic country of ours: some wheat, some greens, some potatoes, some dairy. Father was killed in one a them bizarre industrial accidents farmers are strangely prone to. Jack's daddy went through a potato washer—came out in lumps, apparently. Raw steak with fries on the side—you ever eaten steak tartare? They say human flesh is more like pork, but nonetheless . . .

So, anyway. Daddy went through the wringer; the farm went to the wall. Jack was a college boy, great with numbers but hopeless farmer, didn't have his daddy's touch with the soil. Saw disaster crawling over the hill towards him, black and inevitable. Did everything he could to hold it off, but he didn't have it where it counts. Had to sell the land off, piece by piece. First the arable—Jack was always more of a people person, and a cow's closer to human than a cucumber. Then the pasture, along with those pretty-eyed ladies Jack was so attached to. Cows can be quite attractive, you know, in a big-tits-long-eyelashes kind of a way.

Day the sale went through, Jack watched as his Jersey girls, his daddy's pride and joy, wandered down to the milking shed as usual, into their stalls just like always—only the farm hands hitching 'em up to the milking machine weren't working for him no more. The great cycle of grass, lactation, machinery and cow shit kept right on turning without missing a beat. But he wasn't part of it. He'd never been part of it; he was just some damned idiot who couldn't hang onto what he'd inherited.

He rustled the banker's draft in his pocket and he bit his lip until it bled.

Then he drove into town, found a bar, and got drunk.

Pass that bottle, will ya? I notice you ain't drinkin' yours. Don't worry on my account; I ain't gonna lose it watching someone else drinking my booze. It may or may not surprise you to know I ain't actually an alcoholic. I mean, sure, I've been drunk every time you've been down here, and the first time you found me I was so completely pissy-eyed I could hardly speak, but that ain't because I *got* to be. I just really, really, *really* like to drink. Well, take a look around; living here, who wouldn't? I'm what you might call a *contextual drinker*. Down here, I'll drink every drop I find. But take me outta this particular context you happen to find me in, put me somewhere clean and decent, and I can leave the booze alone with the best of 'em. Although I admit my liver probably don't know the difference.

There's all kinds a drunk, you know. Down here we mostly enjoy the *drinking-to-forget* drunk; although *drinking to stop the voices* is popular too, with a certain discerning clientele. But in the world above the gutter, there's *thousands* of ways to get acquainted with the bottom of the bottle. There's the fun drunk, where the gang's all together and the food's just grand, and everybody's so fuckin' *witty* you can't even believe it. There's the summer-afternoon drunk — ah, that was one a my favourites, back in the day. Sitting with a couple a six-packs, watching the sky and the grass and the water, waking up just as the sun slips behind the hill. There's the *meaningful* drunk, when halfway down the bottle, *damn* if that ain't the secret of the universe, who knew that was it all this time . . . ? Only you can't quite get the cap off the pen, so you have to let it go, and when you wake up the next morning all you can remember is how righteously good it felt to know how the world fits together. The sloppy drunk — sprawled all over your girl, begging her to marry you, so god-damn horny you want to do it right there on the bar stool; only the booze takes all the starch out of you, and she has to carry you upstairs and put you to bed in the spare room. The mean drunk, where you catch a glimpse of your reflection and try starting a fight with yourself. Right now, you and me are having an *educational* drunk — where one of you sits in respectful silence and gobbles up the pearls of wisdom cast before you. So many kinds, so many kinds . . . I gotta take a leak.

That's better. Where were we? Oh, yeah, kinds a drunk. Well, Jackie boy, he went on an *epic* drunk — Homeric in scale. He drank and he drank, and he ranted and raved, and waved his arms around, and stumbled around the room. He was a cabaret, a floorshow, an entertainment all in himself, better'n anything you'd see this year in Stratford, little old England. People actually stayed there to watch him. He did this whole speech on the inequities in the modern capital marketplace that meant that just when you most needed help with your cash flow, all the checks and balances the money men had in place would automatically kick in and prevent you from getting it, and how the perverse incentives of Wall Street would bring the whole system crashing down around our ears one day. Kinda prophetic, huh? Well, when you're looking in the rear-view mirror, everyone's a friggin' genius.

Then he got started on the cows. Took out his wallet, started showing everyone a picture of this one damn cow he'd hung onto. 'This is Genevieve.' Slurring his words, barely able to stand up. Everyone nodding respectfully. 'All I got left — that and an acre of land to graze her on.'

Other end of the bar, there's a guy on a different kinda drunk. He's working his way down a bottle of vodka, shot after shot after shot, not speaking. Their eyes meet in the mirror. Some sort of connection's made.

'Wh'r you?' slurs Jack, sliding onto the bar stool.

The man shrugged.

'I,' he said carefully, 'am a financial wizard. I'm a giant of Wall Street. I've made and lost more money for myself and my employers than you could *dream* of — and I'd trade the whole damned lot for a life I could be proud of.'

Jack gawked.

'I'm drinking,' said the man, every word enunciated with the care of the truly shit-faced, 'because I've just been to the memorial service of a man who used to work for me. He wasn't a *friend*, mind you. He was a salesman; they never have any friends. Just golf buddies and drinking partners. He was killed — by the system.'

'Whatcha talkin' 'bout?' mumbled Jack.

'The system,' repeated the man, calmly. 'The system you were railing against just now. It chewed him up and spat him out, left nothing but a suit of clothes behind.'

'Y're all a shower of bastards,' said Jack indistinctly. 'You and y'r damned rules and y'r freakin' cash flow projections.'

'Indeed, we are. A shower of heartless bastards in expensive suits and red suspenders, and not one god-damned soul between the lot of us. I'll trade you.'

Jack looked blank.

'I'll trade you,' the man repeated. 'I'll trade you that house, and that acre of land, and that pretty-eyed cow of yours.'

'What do I get in return?' asked Jack.

'I'll give you a reco . . . a recomm . . .' the man sighed. 'I'll give you a *recommendation* to my manager, who'll be frantic since receiving notice of my resignation, and desperate for a replacement. I'll call in the morning, give my personal assurance that you're a fine young man, deserving of a chance to prove yourself. Oh, and the keys to my apartment.'

'Yeah, but I don't wanna be like you,' growled Jack. 'Money men took my *farm*, the farm my daddy spent his life building up. There should be a better way . . .'

'Perhaps. But, as you so correctly observe, *we're* all a

bunch of robbers. Who's going to change the world if the good guys won't work for us?'

'What makes you think I'll even be any good?' Jack asked, baffled.

'I have no fucking idea,' said the man, 'and I couldn't care less. But I want out, and you want in. The rent's paid for a month. After that, you're on your own. Deal?'

Jack squinted across the top of his glass.

'Why're you doing this?' he demanded.

The man looked into his vodka and shuddered.

'Because,' he said, 'the system *eats* people. It eats us from the head down, chews us up and discards the empty husks. It is a carnivore, with a predator's instincts, and I do not intend to be its next victim. And since you're so angry and determined and out to get us all, let's see what the system makes of you before it spits out your bones.'

'I'll show 'em all, you know,' said Jack, swaying. 'I'll be decent. Ethical. And if they won't let me, I'll fight the system from the inside, take 'em down. I won't be a corporate whore.'

'Yes, you will,' smiled the man. 'Yes, you will. Here.'

He put a bunch of keys on the bar, then a business-card. *Red Giant Investments Ltd.*

Jack's ticket to board the Money Train.

''kay,' mumbled Jack, and shook the outstretched hand. Then he slid off his stool and passed out.

Was I the Red Giant financial wizard? Ah, just give over, wouldja? Ain't no point trying to work out where I come in this story, 'cos I ain't in it *anywhere*. The men in this story, they're all dead now. Chewed up by the system, leaving nothing but the empty shell behind.

Jack's mother, ah, she was *mad*. Selling off your birthright, completely insane, chasing dreams, not the man your father was, *you* know how it goes. How do I make that out? On account of you wastin' those hard-earned college dollars of yours trailing round the country collecting stories off people like me, that's how. Don't try and tell me your folks are thrilled by the path you've taken . . . anyway, Jackie boy, he shouted her down for once in his life. He was a man possessed; he'd been given a strange, singular chance, and damn, he was going to take it. He packed up his car, his mother and his underwear, and set off to take a bite outta the Big Apple.

New York crashed into Jack like a series of divine revelations, left him gasping and lost. First revelation was the architecture: ornate fingers of glass and concrete that pierced the clouds. He visited St Patrick's to ask for God's blessing on his new life, felt uneasy, couldn't work out why. Finally figured out it was the scale. God's house is supposed to be the biggest place in town, but Wall Street residents bow their heads down at somebody else's altar. When he realised *that*, he had a moment of panic; actually went to Grand Central and looked at the departures board. Looked again at that bit of card in his hand, that ticket for the Money Train.

No contest. The Money Train won. Always does. Jack turned right around and headed back into town.

Second revelation was the apartment. Only four rooms — two bedrooms, living-room with kitchenette in the corner, miniscule bachelor-pad bathroom — but in New York, it's all in the address. His was Ninetieth and Park. His mother looked at the view, and for a blessed minute, she stopped complaining.

Third was the office. He snuck into the building like a thief, convinced he'd be found out. A woman met him in reception, *a certain age* as they say, but damn, she looked good.

'I'm Adela,' she told him. 'You must be Jack.'

'Yes,' he said, thinking to himself, *damn, even the secretaries are hot, all those years I wasted in Idaho . . .*

'You've got a month's trial,' she said. 'You'll report direct to me until we re-staff, picking up where Bradley's team left off. And I warn you, we're up against it. Nick's dead, Ruby's on sick leave, and Brad's idea of a useful contribution is to throw it all up to live in Idaho and send you down here instead.' She looked him up and down. 'So I hope you're everything he said you were.'

'What did he say I was?' asked Jack, busily adjusting his ideas.

'He said you were a bankrupt farmer-boy with a grudge against the system,' she said. Jack nearly swallowed his tongue. 'But he always knew how to spot talent, that man. I guess no-one lasts forever. Come with me.'

Took him into a high glass palace up in the clouds. He had a desk, a phone, a computer, a window, a pile of paperwork, a *compensation package* he didn't even begin to understand, a desk-neighbour name of Jerry. Made some small-talk, him and Jerry getting on famously, and then this — *vision.*

Blonde hair in a chignon, beautiful blue eyes behind thick-rimmed glasses, lovely body in a grey suit, pretty black heels. Only the heels gave her away at first; other than those, she was pure Wall Street, suit with a head on top. But those heels told a different story. Her smile was the other clue; warm and sweet, unexpected.

Jerry caught him looking, grinned.

'That's Aisling Carroll. You know McLain Carroll, right? Red Giant's founding father? She's his daughter, interning for a year. Doing an MBA at Harvard. Waaay too good for us.'

The daughter of the Red Giant, thought Jack, swoonily. *She's beautiful* . . . then, across the office, he saw a huge slab of meat with a shock of red hair, inexpertly crammed into a pin-striped suit by some poor, terrified tailor. The slab glared at Jack like it wanted to kill him.

'That's why we don't mess with her,' said Jerry.

'That's her daddy?'

'Booya.' Jerry lowered his voice. 'You reckon the story's true?'

'What story?'

Jerry looked at him incredulously.

'Where'd you say you were from?'

'Idaho.'

'They have negotiable currency yet in Idaho?' Jack lobbed a pencil over the partition; got it right in the middle of Jerry's forehead, perfect bulls-eye. '*Ow* . . . well, the story goes like this. Mr Carroll got his start at one of the other big places—Lehmann's, I think—then he went out on his own, founded Red Giant from nothing. Grew overnight, just about; man's got the magic touch. Somebody at one of the big firms wasn't happy. One more at the feed-trough means that much less for everyone else, right? So, he decided to take Red Giant down. Him and a couple of other Masters of the Universe, they made a plan. Horned in on his deals, priced him out of the market. Tried to cut off his lines of credit. That kind of thing. Mr Carroll got word of it. Next thing that happens . . .'

Dramatic pause; Jack's eyes like saucers. Jerry glanced over his shoulder, whispered so Jack had to strain to hear him.

'The guy who started it—they found him in the Hudson River.'

'Doing what?'

Jerry laughed shortly.

'Floating, you dimwit.'

'Floating? What—?'

'Face-down. And that isn't the worst part. The worst part—is *all his teeth had been pulled*.' Jack swallowed. Jerry shrugged. 'Red Giant never looked back.'

Jack stared at McLain Carroll, his new boss. Carroll looked back like Jack was next in line for a one-man river-cruise. Jack looked away and shivered.

'Shit. He hates me already.'

Jerry looked Jack straight in the eye.

'Maybe,' said Jerry. 'But he'll leave you alone as long as you bring in the money.'

Jack flicked through the files, gradually realised he was supposed to do a deal with a couple of maverick inventors for the rights to a voice-recognition system for MP3 players. He stared at the pages of figures. And something clicked in his brain.

I can do this, he thought. *I can actually freakin' do this*.

Like I said, the men in this story, they're all dead now.

Course they got to know each other, Jack and Aisling. She was beautiful and outta reach; more than enough to attract him. As for Jack—ah, he had that farmer-boy physique, the build that comes effortlessly when you work on the land. In that polluted corporate ocean, he stood out like a tall ear of corn: strong, golden, and totally outta place. Plus, as it turned out, they both had this fantastic idea they were going to be *good*. Shared dream; bringing ethics to Wall Street. How could they resist?

First, the high-octane business discussions, the junior staff all working crazy hours, Aisling and Jack fitting in nicely. Meeting by the coffee percolator, nothing planned; just more often than not, come break-time there they'd both be. Next, that wilful blindness; you both act like it's all still spontaneous, but still, a lull in the working day and God *damn*, there you both are again, what are the *odds*? All the rest of the percolator crowd getting wise to it, staying out of the way; Jerry giving way last of all, a bit jealous, a bit reluctant to concede defeat. Then, the first time you slip over into the edge into personal . . .

Why are you here? she asked him, one hot October night. *You seem far too . . . nice.* So he told her the story he hadn't even told Jerry: the farm in Idaho, the shame of losing his birthright. *I want to do better than they did by me,* he said earnestly. *I want to make the money-men play fair.*

She looked at him like she'd just seen him properly for the first time.

So why do you *do it?* he asked her. *Why work so hard? With your dad running the place and all?*

She blushed like a rose. He felt his heart squeeze with it.

That's why I have to work so hard, she told him. *I've got to . . .* she sighed, and pushed her glasses up her nose. *I've got to* earn *it.*

You can fall in love with the smallest damned things. Jack fell for the way she looked when she pushed those glasses up her nose. Just that, and he was a goner. He kissed her, soft, innocent; felt like he was drowning. She let him, for just a second, then pushed him away.

'No,' she said, her face little-girl serious. 'I don't do office relationships.'

But he could hear her breathing faster; he knew that, with time, with patience, she'd be his.

Could have been happy, too, if they'd met on any other

street than that one. But as it was, the Money Train was already at the station, the porter beckoning them aboard.

You ain't married. No, I ain't asking a question, I'm telling you, fact: *you — ain't — married*. How do I know? Cuz you're down here at one in the morning drinking with a homeless guy, that's how. So you won't know what it's like to build a life together. Jack and Aisling, a pigeon pair of starry-eyed dreamers. She wouldn't even date him till she went back to Harvard, and when they did get started, they took it slowly. Both afraid of damaging this precious, fragile thing growing between them. They finally fell into bed together one glorious Spring afternoon when Jack got his first promotion. Ah, they came fast to him then; Wall Street's good to its golden boys.

Still they kept it quiet, hiding where no-one from Wall Street ever looked. Took the boat to see the Statue of Liberty, holding hands like teenagers. Went up the Chrysler, took in a view even better than the one from Red Giant's offices. Rode the subway to Coney Island, Jack winning and winning on the shooting galleries.

The monster in the closet was Mr Red Giant, who still didn't know Jack was slipping around with his daughter. Coupla nights Jack actually woke up in a cold sweat, dreaming of deep water filling his lungs. But by that time, the little ole farmer boy from Idaho was an established asset to Red Giant, a lead producer, bringing home the bacon time after time, and they rewarded him accordingly. First an office, then a corner office, all the time that *compensation package* creeping upwards and upwards. Then a suite with its own bathroom attached. Can't have the reigning monarchs pissing in the same urinals as the aspiring heirs; one of those hungry little suckers might just reach over and chop his dick right off. You think I'm joking, dontcha? Easy to see *you* ain't never ridden the Money Train . . .

Ah, the Money Train; God help us all, the Money Train. First you hear the scream of the whistle, so loud it hurts your ears. Then there's this — unearthly *thing* — twice the height of a man, and maybe a hundred feet long, thundering towards you, grabbing the air right outta your lungs, sucking you into its path so you have to hold onto something. It rolls into the platform, you think, *Man, that's the scariest thing I ever saw.* You look at the wheels, the steam, the sweating men shovelling coal. Looks like one of Lucifer's angels, sent forth from the gates of hell to claim you.

Then the door opens and there's a man waving you on, and damn if that ain't a ticket in your hand.

You pat the red velvet seats as you sit down; *just a few stops*, you think to yourself, *then I'll get off.* You can't quite believe it when the wheels start turning, and *man*, what a rush. You take your turn shovelling coal; brutal, backbreaking work, so hard you can hardly take it, but it's worth it, because you know what's coming up. And then you take your break in the restaurant car, and you just can't believe you made it, they invited you in, you're sat right here on the Money Train with the crisp linen napkins and the bottles of champagne. *Just a few stops*, you think again. *Just a few stops and then, I swear, I'll get off.*

Then, the scary thing. *You get used to it.* That speed, that noise, it starts to seem *natural.* You get used to the heat, the swaying motion, the world going by in a blur. You remember how it feels to be one of those folks at the level-crossing, forced to stop while the Money Train goes by, and you like the feeling. The whole world stops for you! People bring you stuff on silver platters, the prices are insane, but hell, who cares, right? You're on the Money Train! Who gives a shit about the mark-up?

And before you know it, the Money Train's got you good. Ain't no way you're getting off, not until the Money Train's taken everything you've got, not until the man in the uniform comes by and says, *Hey, buddy, this is your stop.* You want to stay on longer, but it ain't never been your ride; someone else was working the strings the whole time, figuring out when to shove you back out into the cold. The whole infernal contraption screeches to a halt and the porter flings open the door and tosses you out. And then you're standing on the platform in a cloud of smoke, watching the train roll out again, and you're poorer and older and dirtier, stood someplace you never intended on going, and you can finally see again how fucking insane the whole thing is—but the Money Train don't care. It just rolls on and on, out of the station, taking the next poor suckers on to the end of their personal line.

So where did it all go wrong for Jack and Aisling? They started out with such high hopes, such magnificent fuckin' ideals. But there ain't nobody alive can reform the Money Train; it gets to everyone in the end. And then one night, Jack met Charlie. After that, it was only a matter of time: Doomsday clock at the station counting down, counting the hours and minutes and seconds till the crash.

Jack and Jerry in a bar in Harlem; two City slickers out on the razzle, celebrating their first truly obscene bonus. Jerry introduced them, maybe just being friendly, maybe trying to drive the thin end of that wedge between Jack and Aisling, who knows? Nobody made him say yes. *Hey, Jack, say hello to Charlie,* said Jerry, and there was no denying the buzz between them, the instant connection.

Five minutes later, they were locked in a cubicle in the men's room, Jack screaming in ecstasy, *Oh, my God, Jesus fucking Christ, that's so fucking beautiful, ohhhh!* and when he came down from the peak, the sound of someone in the next cubicle banging on the wall, *Hey, buddy, you wanna keep the noise down in there?* Jack laughed and banged back, *Whatsa matter, pal, you never been in love?*

Jack and Charlie, lost in each other. He didn't care who heard them together, didn't care about anything. He'd never felt anything like it. She set him on fire; every part of his body buzzed, tingled, sang. He staggered back into the bar, swimmy-eyed and grinning like a madman.

'Pretty good fun, huh?' said Jerry.

'Pretty good fun,' said Jack, in a daze.

Next morning, he couldn't stand to look at himself in the mirror. Had to go to work without a shave, screaming horrors sat on his shoulder, gibbering in his ear. What had he been *thinking*? He was a nice boy, a good boy, raised decent, knew better than to behave like that. Charlie was poison, she was toxic; the deadest of cul-de-sacs. He was meeting Aisling for lunch, their favourite restaurant; couldn't make himself walk over there. Felt like he didn't deserve to be near her. Felt like he wanted to die. Felt like he wanted to see Charlie again, need burned into his brain . . . He pushed the thought away.

He called Aisling, put her off till the evening. Took a company limo down Fifth Avenue to Tiffany's, marched in and laid his sliver of necromantic plastic on the counter. *I want to spend as much money as I possibly can,* he declared firmly, and naturally they obliged. He wasn't the first one, not even the first that day. The clerks at Tiffany's all know when Bonus Time rolls around on Wall Street.

Proposed that night over a criminally expensive meal; she cried as soon as she saw the box. She was a nice girl, but she had the same weakness girls have everywhere — the rainbow flash from a diamond blinds them.

She should have seen that night it was already too late for them. Spending enough on one meal to keep a poor family afloat for a year; beguiled by a rock mined in conditions so obscene they'd neither of 'em have lasted a day there. They'd set out with good intentions, but the system already had its claws in them.

But there ain't nothing so blind as a woman with a ring on her finger. Nothing apart from the man who thinks he's just bought her off with it.

Fast-forward a little. Mr Red Giant's first instinct was to take Jackie boy somewhere nice and quiet-like and get going with the pliers, but they finally came to an arrangement; one thing Jack had learned by now was that just about anything's for sale for the right price. Ole Red laid out Jack's targets for the next quarter, an impossible number that made Jack swallow hard. Then he doubled them. Then he grinned, and tripled them. If Jack made his numbers, Red would consent to the wedding.

Nearly killed Jack, but he did it. The look on Red's face when Jack brought the paperwork — enough to turn milk sour through an iron door.

Wedding of the century, naturally. Tulle and ribbons and decadence; live music and dead guests. Jerry was Best Man; from the look on Red's face, Jack was the Worst Man He'd Ever Laid Eyes On, but Jack was too happy to care.

'I guess I was wrong about New York,' said his mother, sniffing.

'The day you step out of line's the day I kill you,' growled Red, glaring.

'I'd buy a gun and keep it handy,' said Jerry, only half-joking.

'Do you take this woman . . .?' said the priest, on auto-pilot.

'Yes,' said Jack, to all of them. He'd raided the palace and carried off the princess; Red could rant and storm, but Aisling would be in Jack's bed that night. And in the bathroom, while Aisling danced with her daddy, Jack the little laddie was biting his lip and trying to keep quiet as Charlie took him up and up into that high, soaring emptiness only she knew how to help him reach.

Afterwards he leant his forehead on the mirror, staring at his reflection. Flushed cheeks, bright eyes, powered by his pounding heart.

'Never again,' he told himself.

Never again.

The Money Train just kept rolling for Jack and Aisling, deal after deal after killer, impossible deal. After Jack closed on the voice-rec deal, there was the Freedive project—supposed to go to Prickly Tree, but the boss-man topped himself and Jack managed to buy the rights while the company floundered. You ever Freedived, College Boy? Nah, I thought not. Probably only a few thousand people in the whole world can afford it. Little nosepiece that pulls the air right outta the water—damnedest thing you ever saw in your life. After that, some domestic appliance work, dull but profitable. Seems we Americans just can't get enough of our cute little toasters and our adorable little waffle makers.

What, the Freediving thing? Nah, I ain't tried it either. Maybe I ain't even *heard* of it. Maybe I'm just making it up to mess with ya. This is a story, remember, not even my own, just something I heard in a bar one day—you

ain't never getting my tale outta me, College Boy. All I
got for you is Jack's train ride, and its terrible ending.

For a while, you can fool yourself you've got the whole
thing under control. Jack had it all, or so he thought. He
had Aisling; he had the stratospheric career; he had the
swank Manhattan penthouse, the gracious New England
country home, the simple beach-house on the Cape; the
staff, the cars, the use of the personal jet; and if, in that
crazy, sleepless run-up to their wedding day, he'd had
to make the odd deal that didn't live up to the stand-
ards he'd set himself, so what, right? It had all been for
love. And if, over time, he was letting things slip, cutting
corners, squeezing percentages, investing in companies
who weren't as squeaky clean as he'd like, well, he was
still doing a thousand times better than that black-hearted
reprobate lurking at the end of the corridor, screwing
everyone who crossed his path, and all the time watching
and waiting for Jack to step outta line so he could kill him.
Told himself Aisling had it all too: the homes, the lifestyle,
what he'd begun to think of as *a nice little career of her own.*

She wasn't willing to sell out, you see. Still shooting for
the coffee-percolator vision. She gave investment advice
to charities, ethical portfolio, reduced fees, great returns
too. They loved her, swore she was a saint who'd change
the world one day. Jack's take on it? The first time he
made a deal he knew Aisling wouldn't—the first time he
screwed over some poor sucker with a good idea and no
capitalisation—he smiled tolerantly and thought, *Ah, but
it's only because of me she can be so ethical.* Yeah, he actually
let that traitor thought slip past his defences, that *he* was
the one making the sacrifices.

Truth was, he fucking loved it. The power. The terror.
The unbelievable amounts of money.

And, naturally, some of that money went on Charlie.

It began as an occasional thing, just the odd stolen night in the bar. Told himself it was nothing to do with Aisling, nothing that would ever touch her. The lies men tell themselves when they know they're doing something unforgiveable. The next day he'd wake up alone in his bed in the clouds of Manhattan, sweating and cold with the shame of it—and craving her company again.

Just the odd stolen night at first, maybe once a month, maybe less, usually when he and Jerry were really tying one on. A clever girl, Charlie; always knew how to find him. She was an expensive habit, but he could afford her. Hell, he could afford *anything*.

Just the odd stolen night, maybe once a month. Well, maybe over time it was creeping up to two or three times a month, but he could handle that, right? He always picked nights when Aisling wasn't around, didn't want her to see him when he crawled home barely able to speak. Nonetheless, she knew, the way women always know when their man's playing away. She took on a junior—bright young thing she poached from her daddy—made fewer road trips and came home early. Jack tried to act pleased. Truth was, he wanted Charlie so bad he could hardly think straight.

Where to meet her? What was the smallest risk? He could meet her in a bar—but then going home to Aisling afterwards . . . Could smuggle her up to his office, but the risk of Red catching them . . . Or go to a hotel—yeah—that could work—

He engineered a fake trip away, meticulous planning, conscious all the time that ole Red was watching, waiting, with murder on his mind. Would you believe Jackie boy hadn't never booked a hotel room his whole life? First he was too poor, then he was too rich. But he found a nice place in mid-town where the concierge understood. Cash payment, and no questions about visitors who didn't check in at the front desk.

Spent the night in Charlie's arms; didn't sleep a wink. Dragged himself into the office the next morning like a walking corpse.

'You all right, boss?' his secretary asked.

'Fine,' he muttered. Staggered into the bathroom and threw up.

The lies men tell themselves.

After that, there was no chance he could keep it under control. Charlie was on his mind the whole time, every minute, every second. He met her in airports, in hotels and bars; every business trip he took, Charlie was along for the ride. He craved her constantly. Aisling had been talking about a baby, but naturally there was no fuckin' chance of *that* happening; Charlie took all his energy. Blamed it on pressure of work, then when she asked him *tell me about it, maybe I can help*, he got angry and yelled at her to *get off my back, damn it, what the hell would you know about it with your fucking* charity work *and your*—then hated himself for the look on her face.

Thing was, he really *was* feeling the pressure. Work was harder now, the money not so easy to find, holes starting to appear in the numbers. His particular trip on the Money Train was reaching its end; it was nearly time for the porter to open the door and toss him out. The deals were tougher to make—or maybe they just seemed tougher, maybe he was losing his touch. By now he was doing the one thing he'd sworn he'd never do—smuggling Charlie up to his plushy office, getting it on with her right down the corridor from Red, looking at his hands shaking afterwards as he tried to pour the coffee and thinking, *Shit, this really has to stop, she's going to kill me . . .* and she wasn't a cheap mistress to keep either; she was the best of the best, his Charlie girl, the cream of the fucking crop. Had to take short-cuts to keep it all going, dancing around the edges of the law. Then he had to stop dancing and start walking, all the way over that line and down, down, down into the murky world of *corporate malfeasance*. Screwing over the people he was investing in. Juggling money. Hiding losses on one deal with profits from another, moving the hole around, hoping he'd find a way to fill it before someone caught on. Sometimes he came home sweating with fear at the thought of the secrets he was hiding; the things he'd done; the stuff he'd stolen; the damage he was doing; the lives he was destroying.

But he was on the Money Train, and he didn't know how to get off. Just knew he was heading for an almighty crash. He saw it coming; but there wasn't nothing he could do. If you'll forgive me an abrupt change in my metaphorical direction—even the world's lousiest farmer knows that eventually, your chickens come home to roost.

You got any more in that bottle?

Hmmm. Ain't nothing like the burn of a quality Scotch whisky.

No, I am not avoiding the fucking subject. Stop tryin' to *analyse* me, you sanctimonious prick, or you're gonna see my ugly side. You know *nothing* about me, College Boy, and you never will. That's the one fearful beauty of this godforsaken shit-hole: *nobody knows who you really are.*

The last day of Jack's life began like any other. He and Aisling were barely speaking by now, barely even *meeting*, just lying in that cherrywood sleigh-bed, back to back,

Jack counting losses and wondering how much longer he could hide it from Ole Red, and Aisling—ah, ain't a man anywhere knows what a woman thinks about at a time like that, and I'm no fuckin' different. Sometimes Jack heard her crying. Couldn't see how to make it stop.

So it was a shock to hear Aisling's voice in his assistant's office. *I don't care* what *he's doing in there, Beatrice, I'm his* wife. *I need to see him. Right now.* And Beatrice doing her best to stall her: *Mrs English, ma'am, I do know who you are, of course I do, I just really don't think—*

Trapped in his office with Charlie, his wife at the door. Like a moment in a nightmare. No way out.

The door opened.

Close your mouth, boy. Lotta flies down here.

Jack had Charlie spread out on the desk, just the way he liked her; he was crouched over her, eyes half-closed, face flushed, futile attempt to hide her.

His wife, his beautiful angel wife, staring at him. In her hand, a bundle of papers spelled D-O-O-M in the reddest of inks. She'd come to save him from Ole Red's wrath, convinced her daddy had it wrong. But for all his faults, Red was never wrong about the money; Aisling was finally seeing the truth. End of the Money Train. End of the line.

'God help me,' whispered Jack.

Aisling looked at him. At his face. At his hands. At the six rows of white powder Jack had chopped out in front of him. Finally understood.

'Cocaine,' she said softly. 'All this time I thought—I thought you were with—and it was—' Her face was white. 'Oh, Jack, Jack—' Trying to hold it together. 'And these papers—these deals . . .' Tears pouring down her cheeks.

'It's not what it looks like,' said Jack, ridiculous, because how the hell *else* could the situation be construed? He'd ruined himself, destroyed his marriage, damned near bankrupted Red Giant. He was a junkie, a thief, an embezzler and an all-round bastard; everything he'd sworn he'd never be.

'Yes, it is,' she said. 'It's exactly what it looks like, Jack.' She held out the papers; her hands were shaking. 'And *this* is what it looks like too. These things you've done. This missing money.'

'No,' he whispered.

'Yes,' she said. 'Nobody can think straight when they've got an addiction to feed. Oh, Jack—'

She wiped tears off her chin with the back of her hand, and pushed her glasses up her nose. 'I thought it was a mistake,' she said. 'I thought, *My Jack, there's no way he'd do this—he might fall in love with someone else, but not lying—not stealing—this is a mistake*—but there is no mistake, is there, Jack? Jerry was right. It's all true.'

'*Jerry?*' The name like a slap in the face. Even when your insides are black and numb with the bad things you've done, you can still feel the pain of betrayal. 'That little bastard, I'll—'

'My dad made him check, he was getting suspicious—he tried to *save* you, Jack. He called me before he sent it, so I could warn you—'

'You came here to *warn* me?' Her goodness in his heart like a bright knife. 'You thought I was cheating on you, and you still came here to warn me?'

'I thought there was still a chance to save us,' she said. 'But there's no point, is there? There's nothing to save. You're not the man I thought you were. We were going to change the world, remember? And now you're worse than any of them.'

Jack stared at her, groping for the words. Couldn't find them.

Then he heard this almighty roar, more like an animal than anything that ever wore clothes. Heard Beatrice scream. Then McLain Carroll, the Red Giant himself, exploded into the room.

'*You*,' growled Red. 'You fucking little thief. Thought you could put it all right, did you? Thought you could put the money back before anyone noticed?' Jack saw his hands twitch. 'I've been waiting for this moment since your wedding day, you asshole. I told you then I'd kill you if you ever stepped outta line — I've been fucking *praying* for the chance to do this —'

'No!' screamed Ashling.

Red was quick, but Jack was quicker, and coked out of his head into the bargain. He reached into his desk drawer. Pulled out the gun Jerry told him to buy.

For a moment, the universe stopped. Jack remembered his wedding day, how Aisling looked when he lifted her veil; the first time he kissed her, that night by the percolator; how his shirt stuck to his back when he first walked in off the street into the air-conditioned office; the way the sun looked coming up over the hill at the back of his daddy's farm in Idaho, spilling over the horizon like corn syrup.

Then he pulled the trigger, and shot McLain Carroll right through his old black heart.

He and Aisling looked at each other over the body of her father.

'I'm sorry,' he told her. 'You're right. I'm not the man we both thought I was. Every word you said is true.'

She stared at him wordlessly, her father's blood pooling around her feet. Too much happening in too little time. A crash always seems to happen in slow motion.

'I'm not as strong as you,' he said. 'I never was. It was all too much for me. I'm so sorry, Aisling. For what it's worth, there never was another woman. I *always* loved you.' He held the gun to his head.

'Don't—' she said, on a reflex.

'I think you should go now,' he said. 'I need to pay the bill. This is the end of the line for me.'

She would have stayed, to be with her daddy if nothing else, but Beatrice grabbed her by the arm and dragged her to the elevator, fast as they could go.

But not far enough to get away from the sound of that second gunshot.

Bottom of the bottle, pal; end of the line. The Money Train stopped, threw all the Red Giant employees out at the station. Jack had done what he'd always said he'd do, after a fashion: he'd brought down one of the giants of Wall Street from the inside. Company went to the wall. Aisling buried her father. Jerry died in a car crash.

What the heck you talking about, *What happened to Jack?* You got all the pieces, pal; you can't put together a suicidal coke-head who just shot his father-in-law and a gunshot in a deserted office, you ain't any kind of a storyteller.

Sheesh, once you get an idea in your head . . . look, even if there was a way for him to get outta that office—d'you think I'd tell you if I *was* Jack? Think I'd admit to being that sorry excuse for a man? Think I'd confess on tape to embezzlement and murder? I told you, College Boy, I ain't in this story anywhere. The Money Train crashed, and took Jack down with it; I just crawled out from the wreckage. I'm just a travelling pilgrim, hiding out in this City of Angels, doing penance for all my sins, till I can finally hitch a ride outta here in an empty railroad car.

Interview #27

—Ruth Boone
Hollywood, Los Angeles, CA

THE THING ABOUT Private Investigators: our stories belong to other people. We're voyeurs by nature. We watch Life sashay down the street, ripe and lovely and sinful and sweet, while we lurk in the shadows and pick out the flaws. Tinseltown's harshest critics are its PIs, turning the icons of our age back into the ordinary flesh and blood they secretly always knew they were.

Of course, a PI only spills what she sees to whoever's paying the bills, and even then she uses her head and knows when to shut up. Too many answers can drive you mad. I can't tell what I know to any bright-eyed travelling man who crosses my path in a bar. That said, I think I've got a tale for you, although all names have been changed to protect the innocent. The innocent, and the guilty, and the ones who are just living their lives, doing the best they know how. Of course, it all depends on how you define *best*.

It starts the way these things always start: with a phone call. I'm drinking Jack Daniels in the Manderley bar, watching the sunset and the bartender. She's a hot little Latino number, sweet and simple and satisfying, like ice-cream swirled with caramel sauce. The man beside me watches too, but it's me she smiles at from beneath her eyelashes. I imagine taking her to an island in the sun for a long, slow vacation. She'd kick off her shoes and dig her toes into the sand, and her curls would shine with coconut oil . . .

Then my phone rings, and I sigh and take the call, because I'm between jobs right now, and God knows I could use the money.

'Yes?' I've still got half an eye on the girl. She's mixing a Seabreeze; there's a scar at the base of her thumb.

'Ruth?'

I'd like to order a Seabreeze and watch her mix it for me. Maybe hang around till she gets off shift, persuade her home with me. We'd dance slowly to Sinatra and talk until the sun came up . . . 'If you've got this number, you know it's me.'

'I know, I'm just messing with ya. Turn around.'

I turn around and see my least favourite conjunction of carbon atoms five feet behind me. He snaps his clamshell shut and saunters over.

'Very fuckable,' he says, nodding to the bartender. This is Angel Pulanski's idea of building rapport, which probably explains why his girlfriends charge by the hour. 'Heard you were short of work.'

'Did you?' He's right, of course. Hollywood's like that, for PIs as much as anyone. Some months you're under the money-tree in blossom season. Others, you're selling CDs to make rent.

'Got a job for you.' His teeth are the only non-grubby part of him. The contrast beween the white veneers and the face around them is terrifying.

'I don't work for trash.'

'*Hush Hush* ain't trash. We got awards.'

'Who says I was talking about the magazine?'

Pulanski's the Teflon man when it comes to insults.

He hitches himself onto a barstool. I took an assignment from him three years ago, a scam the local Precinct had going with the working girls, letting them work the streets in peace in return for services rendered. A good piece of work that needed doing. Pulanski refused to run it because, get this, the girls weren't pretty enough. Swore I'd never work for him again.

'Kate Miller. One a my boys saw her in this *intime* little shithole the wrong end a Sunset, meeting some guy.'

'So?'

'I want photos.'

'You've got photographers.'

'Yah, well, I also got a deal with her husband. He lets me on set to report all the dirt he don't feature in. He knows all my boys and girls, and they ain't as good as you at sneaking around. He sees 'em tailing Kate, I'm dogmeat, you know what I'm sayin'? But if it just lands on my desk . . .' He grins. 'Even the King can't argue with the First Amendment.'

No way is this all of the truth. For whatever reason, Angel's pissed at Brad, and he wants revenge.

'What's he done to get under your skin?' Angel looks shifty. 'Come on, Angel, spill.'

'If I tell you will you take the job?'

'No chance.'

'Then I ain't telling.' He winks. 'You gonna make rent this month?'

'I'll sell my Louboutins.'

He glances down. My shoes are butter-soft caramel suede with luscious four-inch heels, and I can feel every step of the short walk from the lot to the bar throbbing in the soles of my feet. They're beautiful shoes, but they're breaking my heart. Much better to end it now, before I get too involved.

'Think you'll get five thou for those? Cuz that's what I'll pay.'

'Dollars? Or pieces of silver?'

'You want it as *twenty thousand quarters*?' He sighs. 'Well, okay, but are you fucking nuts?'

'Forget it. No deal, Angel.' I slide off the bar stool. My feet protest. I ignore them.

'Fair enough.' I don't like Angel's smile. 'Brad King's got the best security in Hollywood. You'd never get past it, anyway.'

'Are you trying to *needle* me into taking the job?'

'Yeah. Is it working?'

'No.'

'Good. Cuz he'll catch you.'

'I never get caught.'

'Never?'

'Never.' What I mean is *not so far*. But until the day you die, that's the only kind of *never* there is. Angel's laughing, because he knows he's found my weak spot.

'Bet?'

'No!'

'Betcha three thou?'

'You said five, you sly bastard.'

'Damn. So I did. So you'll do it for five?'

Over his shoulder, the bartender's laughing with a customer. Five thousand. Five months of rent; a week in the Caribbean; five year's worth of Seabreezes. It's not the most I've made off a job, but it's the most for a while. On the downside, I hate Angel.

'I still hate you.'

'That's okay, I hate you too. We got a deal, though, right?'

I hold out a hand and try not to shudder when he takes it.

That night I change into black silk pyjamas, pour myself a whisky and sit down with a pack of Red Apples and three DVDs from the corner store. *The Crystal Necklace. The Alabaster Ring. The Golden Cradle.* I watch them with half an eye and rummage through my near-perfect collection of *Variety, Hello!, Hush Hush* and *National Enquirers,* tracing Kate's transformation from coltish unknown to full-blown superstar, wife of her producer and co-star Brad King. Her talent and her heart-stopping beauty are the only reasons *Necklace* survived its opening weekend. Kate put Brad back on top with three back-to-back gold-plated hits, then made him a father into the bargain. There's the iconic shot in *Hello!,* taken a year ago: Brad protective, Kate glowing, baby Miranda wary and curious, huge eyes and hair like thistledown. Brad, inevitably: 'Miranda's the most beautiful thing I've ever seen.' I have to disagree. I don't really like babies and, actually, Kate Miller is the most beautiful thing I've ever seen.

I freeze on a close-up of her exquisite face.

The next day, the temperature's rising. I call around a few contacts, find the company that supplies the Kings' cleaning staff. They're supposed to be security-checked, but LA's a border town full of drifters; the companies swear blind they're on top of it, but they're all liars. A quiet conversation and a fistful of dollars, and I'm walking in through the service door with a mop and bucket in my hand.

A maid's uniform is like an invisibility cloak. I roam the mansion, opening doors and doors and more doors, until I find Kate's PA's office. She's in it, but she's on the phone, and she waves me in and carries on talking, pacing up and down. I mop the floor for a while, deliberately getting in her way. After she falls over me for the fourth time, she gives me a look and disappears into the corridor, shutting the door.

Since I don't want to get my contact into trouble, I finish mopping, dust the shelves and empty the trash. Then I riffle through the desk and find a diary with wall-to-wall appointments, great and small. Beauticians, trainers, hairdressers, stylists, journos, shutterbugs, personal shoppers. I can hear the assistant pacing in the corridor outside and make with the mop, sloshing warningly around.

Then I find it: two days later, a tell-tale gap in the schedule, a pause in the merry-go-round. A three-hour window in time, through which I can spy on Kate's long lunch with Nobody.

Bingo.

Kate leaves via the service entrance, driving herself in a beige SX4. From the way she watches the mirrors, it's clear her biggest worry is her own security team. Five minutes out from the house and she plainly doesn't have five husky guys with a lot of bling tailing her, so she relaxes. She doesn't flinch at the 'SEE THE HOMES OF THE STARS' minibus; it's empty, and the driver's kicking back and drinking a milkshake. I put the drink on the seat beside me and stay two or three cars behind.

We're heading into the hills. After a while I guess where we're going, and take a chance and a short cut. By the time she arrives at the Hollywood Observatory, I'm comfortably nestled down among the scrub, my camera trained on Kate and a skinny, out-of-town-looking guy chewing his fingernails.

I can't hear what they're saying, so I watch the body language. There's intimacy, but not that kind; I'm pretty sure they're not sleeping together. He's asking for something. She's refusing, but she doesn't want to piss him off too much either; the power dynamics are strange here. Looks more like blackmail than anything else. I triple-check the flash is off, squeeze off a few shots. Anywhere else, the guy would be passable — a bit skinny, but he has nice dark eyes, thick black hair — but in Tinseltown, he's got *loser* tattooed on his forehead. No presence on camera. Kate, unsurprisingly, photographs like a dream. However, she's wearing no make-up. She'll be beautiful till she dies, but pretty is mostly grooming, and today, she isn't the least bit pretty.

He glances up and I flinch. The camera's painted matt black and the lens is shielded, but sometimes the sun catches it at the wrong angle . . . I squeeze off one more anyway, get a shot of him looking warily upwards. He's getting angry. So is she. She's snarling now, her face contorted with passion. He grabs her arm. She shakes it off, but not in the incredulous way we do when a stranger touches us. There's the weariness of familiarity about them. Interesting. The argument ends with Kate storming off, but she hesitates as she goes and it's clear that, whatever it is, it's not over.

Kate Miller is definitely not sleeping with this guy. They know each other to the bone, but there's about the same amount of lust as I have for my little brother. I doubt Angel would pay fifty bucks for these shots; no matter how he cuts them, it doesn't add up to *Screen Siren's Secret Love Tryst!*, which is the headline he's looking for.

So — what?

I can't afford to be curious, but sometimes you have to splurge. I watch him all the way back to his car. It's a Hertz rental, narrowing it down to just under thirty per cent of all rented cars in the State, but I've got a make and model, and an ex-girlfriend at the office, and I reckon I can find the guy's name.

'Whatever you want, Ruth, it's no,' Carolina says when I lean across the rental desk and smile. Not a good start. 'Nice shoes, by the way.'

'What makes you think I want anything? And thank you.'

'Because that's the only time you come around,' she says wearily, pushing her hair back from her forehead. 'And I was up all night with the baby and I'm tired and I'm not in the mood.'

'I didn't know you and Jennifer—' I bite my tongue, but it's too late.

'That's because you never come around except when you want something. Didn't you notice I was pregnant last year?'

I think back. Last year was the Flores case—a high-schooler who faked a trip to the Grand Canyon. He had it all worked out, called when he said he would, friends sending postcards for him at strategic points. Only thing he hadn't allowed for was good old Uncle Pete trying to meet him for dinner. I found him in Atlantic City. He was running an online gambling company from the school library; he'd gone to meet his backers. Carolina helped me track his rental car. I remember thinking she'd put some weight on, and that it suited her.

'That's so like you.' She shrugs. 'I'm happy, I don't need you, so I'm invisible. All your attention goes on your work.'

It's nothing but true, which makes it worse.

'I'm sorry.' She takes my hand remorsefully. 'That was mean.'

I don't want her to see me hurting. But I don't have anything else to use.

'How sorry?'

'Ruth, for God's sake . . .' she laughs. 'You're unbelievable, you know that?'

I keep looking at her. It's not in Carolina to say 'no' to anyone. That kid of theirs will grow up more spoiled than a tub of warm yoghurt.

'Okay,' she sighs. 'Hit me with it, Ruth.'

And now I'm walking away from the rental office, and I'm definitely not crying, because that's just not my style, and I've got a name. Thomas Anderson. I've prostituted myself for two words on a Hertz-branded sticky-note. I wonder if there's a way to calculate *self-esteem*, bill it as an expense item to Angel.

It's late that evening. My living room's filled with dirty glasses, cigarette butts, paperwork and other people's personal business. I pick up a highball with a dried-up lime wedge in the bottom, then put it down again. Why pick on that one thing when there's so much else to go at?

Thomas Anderson is an insurance manager from Wisconsin, which makes him a damned long way from home. I look again at the photos, wondering how he knows her, what he is to her. Sweet Jesus, she's beautiful. Even when she's screeching like a banshee, she's beautiful. I'm watching *Necklace* for the fourth time.

Something's nagging me, and I just can't figure out what. What have I looked at that I haven't seen? What have I heard that I haven't listened to? I'm tired; it's been a long, strange day, and I'm not proud of my part in it. Before I can stop myself, I remember Carolina's face. *I was up all night with the baby*. Damn babies, everywhere babies, I swear the world would be better without them . . .

And then I'm leaping out of my seat, riffling through the photographs, and it's staring me right in the face, and I'm furious because I hate being wrong, but at least I'm the only person who knows how wrong I was. On the upside, I'm now sitting on a goldmine, a story big enough to keep me in anything I want for the next ten years; Angel will have to pony up a lot more than five grand to get his hands on this one. On the downside, if I take the money, I'll be worse than Angel's ever been.

I have a decision to make.

I'm sliding on my belly through the undergrowth, freezing, when the guards pass, peeling off an entire outer layer of clothing and hiding it in the California lilac so I can go in clean and leave no trace, jimmying the French doors to Kate's bedroom. Kate and Brad are at the premiere of *Lost in Vegas*. There's no intruder alarm; this place is more like a hotel than a home, and more like a prison than both. I slide through the gap and hold my breath for thirty seconds. But nobody hears me. I've cut my hand, but I'm feeling no pain; I'm high as a kite on adrenaline. I wrap it in a strip of my discarded outer T-shirt. I can't afford to leave bloodstains.

Her room's beautiful, minimal to the point of emptiness, a style only sustainable for those with infinite closet space and an army of minions to pick up after them. But there'll be something, I know it. Women always keep souvenirs. Beneath my bed, I have a scruffy cardboard box with letters, photographs, a blue T-shirt stiff with seawater. It's poorly hidden, but I have no-one to hide it from. Kate has maids, security guards, a jealous husband, plus her own personal staff, because a secret like this would break the loyalty of anyone.

Human beings measure time by the beat of their heart. It seems an age I'm in there, but Mr Seiko tells me it's only been thirty-five minutes when I find what I'm looking for: a legal-sized envelope taped to the back of the erotic Hiroshige print above her make-up stand.

Leave now, my heart tells me, pounding and pounding. *You've got at least twenty minutes*, Mr Seiko insists. I can't listen to my heart; what's in the envelope can't leave this room. I tip the contents onto the bed. I'm expecting the letters, but not the yearbook, which falls open at a page two-thirds through.

There's Kate, younger and fresher, her hair in a pony-tail, her make-up inexpert and smeary. And there's Thomas Anderson, beside her on the bleachers, those eyes piercing me, wary and watchful. I'm transfixed. There he is. There they are. Kate Miller and Thomas Anderson.

The handle of the door turns.

But you had time, insists Mr Seiko, ticking like thunder. *Told you to take it with you*, my heart screams, *now we're screwed, aren't we?* There's nowhere to go. Even if I had time to make the window, which I don't, there's no way to replace the evidence. *I never get caught.* But until the day you die, *never*'s only *not so far*, and the way my heart's clawing its way out of my chest, that day could be today — Kate limps into the room, wearing a demure and simple white sheath dress. The boat-neck caresses her immaculate collarbone, the sleeves cover her elbows but stop short of her wrists. Her hair is a heavy chignon, tendrils coiling onto her neck. Her nude peep-toe Manolos and her perfect French pedicure make me feel underdressed. She drops her purse, pulls off the heavy diamond ear-rings and snatches off her shoes in one continuous gesture of disgust that flows seamlessly into the moment when she looks up and sees a strange woman, hair shoved under a woollen hat and dirt under her fingernails, riffling through her most intimate business.

I can't begin to imagine how she must feel.

We stare at each other. I watch her pass from amazement to terror to horrified understanding. She subdues her instinct, which is to scream. My heart has taken all the pain it can tonight; I don't think it can cope with watching her silence, the mark of her isolation.

'It's all right.' The words come up out of my gut; my brain gets no say in it. She shakes her head, and she has a point; how can it possibly be all right?

'You're press,' she whispers. 'That guy in the diner . . .'

I cross the room and take her hands in mine. They're impossibly silky and soft. I think about the hours that go into their care: creams, hot towels, massages. My bandage smears her fingers. 'My name's Ruth Boone and I'm a Private Investigator. And I can help you.' A scream bubbles in her throat. I have to silence her, for her sake as well as mine. My mouth finds hers before I even know what's happening. Her lips part for me, I taste her tongue against my own. What am I doing? We're both trembling when I pull away.

'How can you help?'

I can hear voices in the corridor outside. Someone will be here in seconds to help her out of that dress, to return the jewellery to the vault. I have fractional moments to find the right words. My brain finally decides to help out.

'I can help you with Miranda's father,' I tell her.

I sit in my living room and watch the sunrise. It's a sad fact that even the dawn can look worn-out seedy when it struggles to reach you through a haze of cigarette smoke.

What have I done?

'His name's Thomas Anderson,' I tell Angel, over an espresso brought by his assistant. I don't drink it, on the somewhat flawed principle that, when wilfully withholding the story of the decade from the man paying your fee, the moral thing to do is to take as little else from him as possible. 'They were at high school together. No romance. Just catching up on the past. Bad luck.' Every word I tell him is true, but *truth* and *honesty* are more distantly related than you'd think. I hand him the photographs, minus one.

'I see . . .' Please God, he won't see. 'Krabitz, get your ass over here.' A skinny guy eating cold noodles out of a box ambles over. 'This the guy?'

Krabitz looks. 'Yeah, that's him.'

'Fucking hell.' Angel glares at me, like it's my fault his mark isn't having sex with a Wisconsin insurance salesman. Part of him wants to let go; he's already pissed away five grand on nothing. But the bigger, hungrier part still hopes. He taps his fingers against the glossy paper.

'How about you tail her a bit longer? I'll pay three a week for the next five weeks. You never know, right?'

'What did Brad King do to piss you off?'

'He cheats at poker, the little shit. You gonna follow Kate for me?'

'This is about *poker?* No deal.'

'Why? My money not good enough for you suddenly?'

'I'm telling you, Angel, there's nothing there.' A huge lie, my first. Already Kate Miller is corrupting me.

'Everyone's guilty of something.'

'Let it go, Angel. The story you wanted isn't there. And it's against my code of conduct to exploit my clients.'

'A PI with morals? I'll call the taxidermist.'

'Did you just use a four-syllable word? I'll get him to stuff you while he's here.'

He grins, and looks me up and down. It's a long way from amicable.

'Okay. You win. We'll call it quits at five. Nice shoes.'

'Thanks. Nice veneers.'

'Thanks. Don't fall off those heels on your way out.'

It's three days later and I'm staring at a cheque for five thousand dollars. The apartment is tidy. For weeks my cupboards will be teetering death-traps and I won't be able to find anything. Apparently a cluttered environment implies a cluttered mind, so what does an empty one mean? My mind is far from empty; it obsessively circles the memory of Kate's mouth like a dog round an empty food bowl.

The knock at the door yanks me out of my chair. I don't know what to do with my hands, or my arms, or my voice. My body has become a strange land. Kate Miller in my apartment is like a unicorn in your bathtub.

'Can you really help me?' Kate begs. It should sound gauche, but beautiful women can break all the rules.

'Yes,' I tell her, this being the one thing I am sure of. 'Everyone has a secret. I'll find his.'

'How did you know?'

I hand her the photo I withheld from Angel; Thomas, glancing warily up at the camera he didn't know was there. She's shocked, as people always are when they find they've been observed.

'I didn't see you,' she says.

'That's the idea.'

'Who paid you?'

'Doesn't matter. They didn't get this.' I remember the

first thought that crossed my mind as I watched them. 'Thomas Anderson is blackmailing you, isn't he?'

'How did you—' She stops. 'Yes, he is.'

'But it's not for money.'

'No.'

'Access? To Miranda?'

A tear rolls down her cheek. If I touched my tongue to its path, would the taste be salt or sweet?

'I'm so scared,' she whispers. 'If anyone, anyone sees them together—'

'Tell me how it happened.'

'You're the detective. If you're so good, you tell me how it happened.'

Kate needs a miracle. I need her to believe I can deliver. I begin with what I know.

'You knew him at school,' I say slowly. 'In Silverwood Falls.'

She nods. This much I know from the yearbook, but that's as far as the script goes. I begin to improvise.

'You left him behind when you came to Hollywood,' I say. 'Your father brought you.' She's sceptical, this was in the press coverage. I take a guess. 'Your dad told everyone his daughter would be a star.' I'm looking for the smallest signal, a flicker of an eyelid, a twitch of a pinky finger. Nothing. 'They smiled, but kindly.'

She nods.

'Okay.'

Okay? What does that even mean? 'He parlayed his way past studio security into—into your future husband's office. He made a fool of himself and embarrassed you, but you caught Brad's eye, and he put you into *Necklace*. It was a publicity stunt. There were nasty rumours coming out of the set; he wanted a positive story. Plus, if it flopped, he could blame you.' Too much? I can't tell. 'But it was a huge hit. Because of you.'

'Thank you.'

'We both know it's true.' I can't fit Thomas Anderson into the jigsaw yet, so I keep going. 'Then came *Ring*, lower net but bigger gross, the third one was a cert. Then Brad said for a joke in an interview that if *Cradle* grossed over five hundred mill, he'd marry you.'

'Hollywood romance.' She smiles, but it's brittle. I remember a strange caesura in the *Cradle* coverage that tells me there's a nasty little secret they had to bury. A tiny item from a cub reporter — Kate collapsing on set from 'nervous exhaustion'—which absolutely nobody picks up on. After months of coverage, three weeks of nothing. Sometimes you learn more from silence than words.

'While you were filming *Cradle*,' I try, feeling my way into the sentence, 'you and Brad—'

'It was consensual.'

Has a woman in love ever used the word *consensual*? And then afterwards, she had to marry him. I try not to shudder. This isn't showing me Thomas. I need to look at motivation.

'Walking onto set was like being locked in jail,' I say tentatively. 'Strange people, lights, endless pressure. And Brad, breathing down your neck . . .' At last I've got a reaction; a miniscule flinch she can't restrain. 'The story was you'd had acting lessons since you were six, but nobody came forward and claimed the glory.' Her eyes are huge. 'Kate, did you call Thomas because you needed a friend?'

'He directed me in the high school play,' she confesses. 'He stayed in this god-awful little hotel near the airport, and he visited every single night. He coached me. Thad

Englemann got the Oscar, but they were Tom's films, every one.'

It's too bizarre to be anything but true.

'And . . .'

She dips her head.

'Just once,' she says, from behind her hair. 'After *Cradle* wrapped. I wasn't in love with him, but . . . you know . . .' I do know. 'I was sure the baby was Brad's. Then we did that photo-shoot.'

It's an elusive thing; not colouring, not features. It's the wary way they glance at the camera, the look in their eyes . . . but it's unmistakeable.

'I got the first letter a week later. Can you really make him stop?'

'I already found this much,' I say gently.

'Why would you help me? This story could go for millions.'

'Because . . .' I can't get past *because*. Too many answers to choose from. 'Because . . .'

And then I can't think any more, because she kisses me. Kate Miller kisses me. Kate Miller kisses me, and she's murmuring with pleasure, provoking me to nip her lower lip beneath my teeth. Her frail sweetness, my need to consume and devour, make me think of meringue, and as I lead her to the bedroom where, thank God, the sheets are clean and the ashtray on the night-stand has been emptied, it occurs to me to wonder why I always compare the women I find attractive to desserts, and if this has any bearing on why, ultimately, they always seem to leave me.

Timewipe: a week later. I've driven all the way from Los Angeles to Benton, Wisconsin, to discover that Thomas Anderson is a nowhere man, living in limbo, putting down no roots, leaving no memories. He's been with United Insurance for the last three years, joining from Mid-West Allied. He rents a by-the-numbers-average apartment, in a building you'd struggle to describe even if you lived there. He has three weeks' worth of mail in his mailbox, five pornographic magazines in his closet, a Glock in his sock drawer, for which he has a licence, and every Carly Simon CD ever released. He earns a mid-range salary, wears a suit and tie, and even when prompted with a photo, his co-workers are uncertain who he is. He dates, but is currently single. The one old girlfriend I manage to track down seems bemused by my interest. She murmurs vaguely about a lack of commitment, and is much happier going steady with a fireman. His life reminds me of someone I can't quite place. Somewhere between Benton and Silverwood Falls, I realise it's me, and nearly crash the car in disgust.

Now I'm simultaneously in Silverwood Falls, Kansas, a coffee shop, three-day-old jeans and a vile mood. I'm the only customer, and the lady who pours my coffee smiles warmly and calls me *honey*. I'm tired and convinced I smell. I promised Kate a miracle, and I can't deliver. The photo of Thomas is furry from handling.

'That's Donna Anderson's boy,' says the coffee pot lady. 'Are you looking for him?' She sees the look on my face. 'Welcome to small town life, honey.'

'You know his family?'

'I reckon.'

I can't quite believe what I'm hearing. I've seen this played out a hundred times on the screen. Can it really be this easy? I pat the seat beside me. She sinks gratefully into it.

'They don't live here no more, though,' she continues,

and my heart sinks. 'They moved here from some city, stayed about ten years. Left when Thomas went to college. They was nice people. Quiet, but nice. Mr Anderson, Gregory, he worked at the garage. He was a good mechanic. Donna did a lot for the church. She would have liked more children, but that wasn't God's plan.'

Boring, boring, boring. Literally the only interesting or noteworthy thing that has happened to the Andersons is their son having sex, once, with Kate Miller. It's like their lives were ordered from a catalogue.

'Did they leave a forwarding address?' I have no intention of driving anywhere but home, but she's so nice, I don't want to cut her off.

'Why, not that I know of. I'm sorry.' She really does looks sorry. 'Besides, it was a few years back. They might have moved again.' She rolls her eyes. 'City folk, huh?'

I roll my eyes along with her, even though I myself am a city rat, to the bone. Then I pay my bill and drag myself back to the car, and sit behind the wheel, and light a cigarette, and try not to scream in frustration.

Outside the church a billboard reads, apocalyptically, *The sins of the father shall be visited upon the son a thousand times*. It reminds me why I'm hunting this man. How can he be blackmailing a Hollywood icon for access to their child? A man like this would instruct a lawyer. I stare again at that nice, thick black hair, those dark eyes, glancing warily around for danger where no danger can possibly exist, because who would bother to threaten someone so utterly, painfully bland? It is simply not natural to live a life as blamelessly tedious as Thomas Anderson. *The sins of the fathers*, indeed . . .

And then it comes to me, creeping slyly up my spine and lodging in my brain. The Andersons, materialising from nowhere and vanishing back into the void. Their son, living a carefully rootless existence; a man who has every reason to call a lawyer and nothing to lose. Those eyes; that hair; a sudden escape from an un-named big city. It's a long shot, but this case has been nothing but long shots from the start . . .

My hands shake as I take out my cellular phone.

I have just one person I can call, and even though he's small fry in the organisation he belongs to, he's still the most dangerous person I know. We met in Vegas, working opposite ends of a truly strange incident where a twenty-two-year-old Vegas rookie walked into the Rising Sun Casino, stayed a week, took north of fifty million on the roulette wheel, tipped a showgirl called Alabama twenty per cent and was never seen again. We found Alabama in Toronto, but never managed to turn up anything crooked. Eventually it was written off as one of those painful Vegas episodes, paying for itself in increased revenue from punters who thought next time it might be them. I'd had his number ever since, but had never needed help that badly.

Not until now.

'Ruth Boone.' Mikey Ferracci's charm drips out of the earpiece like poison. 'How you doin'? And where you doin' it?'

'Silverwood Falls, Kansas,' I croak. 'Research.'

'Research is always good. How can I help you with that?'

This is what I remember from our last encounter. That frightening willingness to help. That insinuating desire to weave you into the network of favours.

'I need to show you a photograph.'

There's a fractional pause.

'Ho-kay,' he says. 'Your place or mine, baby?'

'Yours.'

'You flying in? I'll send a car.'

'There's no need—'

'Sure there is. Those taxi drivers, those Armenians, they'll take you to the cleaners. A limo's much more comfortable. Plus, the driver'll know where to find me. I'll send you a car to La Guardia. Really, I insist.'

Those tendrils, you can't escape them. A car. A death-trap. It all depends how you look at it.

'Thank you.'

'No need for thanks. We're partners, right?'

And God help me, I suppose we are.

The driver at La Guardia is groomed and polite, and far cleaner than I am. He takes my suitcase, crammed with dirty laundry, and holds the door for me. I wish the limousine came with a shower. I've flown in on the red-eye, but even if I wasn't wired on coffee and fear, the air conditioning would keep me awake. We drive to a mid-town restaurant. My driver guides me down the steps, his hand in the small of my back like a respectful date.

The man sitting on the other side of the white table-cloth, one hand on a red napkin, one hidden beneath the damask, is a complete stranger.

The driver has to help me into the chair. He brings me a large brandy. I take a mouthful, and wish I had a cigarette.

'Would you like to smoke?' asks the stranger on the other side of the table. A lighted Marlboro appears at my shoulder. I inhale deeply and feel my hands grow steadier.

'Thank you,' I say.

'I apologise for taking Mikey's place,' says the stranger, and smiles. He's large and affable, like a favourite uncle. 'Please, say you'll forgive me.'

'Of course.' It's grotesque, this pretence of manners

when we both know what's really going on here, but I feel compelled to keep up my end of the conversation. 'I hope Mikey's not in trouble.'

'No trouble at all, no trouble at all. He just happened to mention that a good—no, an *excellent*—PI he worked with once was in Silverwood Falls, Kansas, looking for someone. Which was interesting. Because you see, I was in Silverwood Falls myself, six years ago. And I also was looking for someone.'

We regard each other over the tablecloth.

I have to tread very carefully. I know now my long shot is right; the key to Kate's freedom is within my grasp. I just need to get out alive with the answer.

'Perhaps we can help each other,' I say finally. His smile suggests I've just presented him with his first grand-child. Very carefully, I lay down the photo of the man I know as Thomas Anderson on the table between us.

The man looks at the photograph. For a moment, Death himself sits opposite me at the table.

'So,' he says, and the avuncular mask is back in place. 'How can *I* help *you*?'

'I need two things,' I say. 'His name. And twenty-four hours.'

'The name can be managed. The twenty-four hours . . .' he sighs. 'I've wanted to speak to this boy since he was ten years old. His father and I were once very good friends. You understand my dilemma.'

I play my only card.

'My client needs the first shot,' I say. He frowns. They're very careful, always, to use only the most innocu-ous language to outsiders. 'I'm sorry, I mean she needs the first *opportunity*.'

'Perhaps I could speak for your client also,' he suggests

delicately. 'I'd be more than happy to . . . use my influence. As a favour to you.'

'She needs to speak to him personally. It's—a family matter. To do with her daughter.'

This he seems to understand. I see him hesitating. 'You can guarantee he'll be available to me afterwards?'

Now more than ever, I can't lie.

'No, sir, I can't guarantee that.' He looks amused, and raises an eyebrow; he won't say the word, but the twitch of his index finger is enough. How can I say it without saying it? 'Ah, what I mean, sir, is—we expect he'll leave LA after meeting my client. I can't guarantee he'll go home . . . but I can give you his address.' And, of course, his current name. An eye for an eye.

He considers this for a long time. I watch the thoughts unspool behind his eyes. He's thinking Thomas is messing up the future prospects of a starry-eyed Hollywood floweret, and her mother wants to frighten him into leaving her, badly and unheroically. He's weighing up the value of sending the message, *We never forget*, against the value of an LA private investigator in his pocket. He's considering his reputation, his reputation as a good family man. This is all projection. I'm way out of my league. I have absolutely no idea what he's thinking.

'*Women*,' he says ruefully at last. I smile with him. 'And she really won't change her mind on this?'

I spread my hands and shrug.

His eyes, those deep, black eyes with their heavy lashes, look into mine, and I'm grateful that I've spoken nothing but truth since I came into this room. If I'd told one solitary, single lie he would see it in my face, for there is no doubt he is far, far stronger than me. Of course, *truth* and *honesty* are less closely related than many imagine.

Then his right hand comes up from beneath the table,

and reaches into his breast pocket. He removes a fat fountain pen, and gestures to the driver / bartender, who conjures paper from thin air. He writes two words, and folds the paper in half.

'Twenty-four hours,' he says. 'You can contact me via Mikey.'

'I won't let you down,' I say, and he beams at me.

'Ms Boone, I have absolute faith.'

I'm on my knees in the bathroom at La Guardia, dry-heaving into the toilet bowl. I need to stop this, so I can book myself on the first flight back to LAX, then call the rental company and explain what their two-year-old Toyota Camry is doing at Topeka airport. I need to stop this so I can call Kate, and tell her to get Thomas Anderson on the phone and organise a meeting for the second I land, at the airport if necessary. I need to stop this, because I can't convince her of the need for speed at all costs, because after this he'll be gone, if I have to break off every few seconds to vomit. I need to stop this, but I can't. I've never been so terrified in my life. From now on, even after I've delivered on my side of the bargain, I'll be on *their* radar for the rest of my days, that favour I owe them hanging round my neck like an albatross, dragging me down.

The cleaner taps on the door with mulberry gel-tip nails.

'You okay, sista?' she demands.

'Doing just great, sista,' I manage, and hunch over the toilet bowl again.

It's ten hours later, and a nice boy with dreadlocks meets me in Arrivals. It's the second time in two days I've been met by a driver who looks and smells far cleaner than I do, but I'm too exhausted to be embarrassed. Kate waits in the limo, cool and beautiful in a white Armani suit and a silver blouse. She looks shocked when she sees me.

'Ruth, are you all right?'

'Fine. Did you get hold of Thomas?'

'He'll be at the Monkey's Paw in an hour and a half—but why does it have to be tonight?'

I check my watch. I've done this one hundred and ninety-six times since leaving that terrible room in New York. My terror is set on an infallible three-minute timer. Fourteen hours to go. If he's on time, there'll be twelve and a half hours left on the clock. Will it be enough?

'I'll tell you later,' I say. Her perfume is maddening. She pours me a glass of champagne, which I refuse.

'And you've really got . . .' she glances warily at the driver.

'Yes,' I say.

She kisses me quickly on the lips. I must taste vile; I try not to breathe out while she's near me. I rest my head against the seat back and try to doze. Every three minutes, my inner time-demon prods me with his pitchfork and I lurch back into consciousness to check my watch again.

Kate sweeps into the Monkey's Paw like a star, her entourage dispersing around the bar. She's a completely different woman from the harpie at the Observatory, or the lost soul who found me in her bedroom, or the siren who lay in my arms whispering wild encouragement as I drove both of us into oblivious frenzy. I remember, very, very belatedly, that she is an actress.

Thomas sits at the bar, insignificant in the Hollywood light. I wish I could change what's about to happen to him, but it's too late now. Their conversation washes over me like rain. Like a dog, I can only process the tone, and the occasional word. Thomas demanding. *My daughter. I need. Just once. Let me.* Kate pretends to be frightened—*too dangerous*—*if anyone*—*end of my*—*please*—but I can hear it's fake. I check my watch again. Three more minutes off the clock.

'Ruth,' says Kate gently, and I realise I've missed my cue.

'Oh.' I offer the slip of paper. It seems anti-climactic. For a second, Kate hesitates. 'Here.'

She passes it to Thomas. He opens it. I can't breathe.

The colour drains from his face. He shrinks and crumples in upon himself. I think he might actually disappear through the floor. I glance at Kate, to see if she's feeling, as I do, the evil of what we're doing. I wish I was tired enough to miss the glee in her eyes.

'She's *my* daughter,' says Kate, her voice low and clear. 'Never, ever contact me again.' She sweeps out of the bar, hair flying, eyes flashing. It's a magnificent exit. It's my cue to follow her, but I have to do one thing first.

'You need to run,' I whisper. Thomas looks at me speechlessly. 'They'll be coming for you. At your apartment in Benton. You've got—' I check my watch again—'twelve hours and sixteen minutes before they know where you are.' He's a deer in the headlights, and I'm the driver of the forty-ton rig bearing down on him, nothing I can do except mouth *sorry* through the windshield. 'That's as long as I could buy for you. So, run. And never look back.'

Back in the limo, Kate's exuberant. She's played the game and come out on top; her secret's safe; she's still the Queen of Hollywood, the mother of Brad King's daughter. She kisses me, not caring about the entourage, but I'm limp and unresponsive.

'Did you see that? He was completely broken . . .' her laughter is the ugliest thing I've ever heard. 'Oh, Ruth, you're a witch. How did you *do* it? What did I *give* him?'

I look at her for a long time, taking in the shape of the mouth I've tasted, the cheekbones I've caressed, the throat I've kissed. I want to hold onto the beauty, but I can't. Once you've seen the beast beneath the skin, you can't go back.

'What was it?' she repeats.

Too many answers can drive you mad. I want to know what Thomas's father did, who he sold out and what happened after. I want to know if Thomas will escape and keep living his non-life, or if the destiny that has stalked him since he was ten years old will finally find him at a lonely crossroads at midnight. I want to know if Brad King will discover his wife's duplicity. I want to know why she went to bed with me, what it meant to her, and if she'd do it again if I asked her. But every PI has to know when to let go.

'It was his real name,' I tell her.

She looks blank.

'The Mob never forgets, Kate,' I whisper, and close my eyes. Then I jerk awake again, and check my watch. I am more tired than I've ever been in my life, but I have to stay awake for another twelve hours and thirteen minutes. Before I can rest, I have to send a text to a mobile number and thus unleash the Furies upon Thomas Anderson, born Tony Androsciani, whose last known address is an apartment in Benton, Wisconsin.

Interview #42

—Rafael Delgado
New York, NY

I WATCHED THEM SAY goodbye; saw into their souls
you might say, the way I generally can. Two poor, lost
boys, their whole lives bent out of shape by one spiteful
woman with power. Just one good thing: of all the doors
in the mean streets of this city of ours, Paul knocked on
mine.

'I'm so sorry, Snowy,' said Paul. 'I—I—'

'Don't,' I said.

Paul looked at me.

'Leave the kid his heart, at least,' I said, and held the
door open for him.

Of course, that came later on, but I'm starting there,
since that's where I came in. This ain't even my story, to
be honest, not really. I just . . . watched from the sidelines,
advising where necessary.

But for some reason I can't quite fathom, people always
get distracted when they discover they're talking to a
dwarf who strips for a living.

Bet *that* got your attention, right? Now *you're* distracted,
you want to hear about me instead. Tough luck, pal. Like
I said, this is Jakey's story I'm telling.

So; beginnings. Everything has a price in this world,

and some things come more expensive than others. About nineteen years ago—when I'd finally accepted I'd never be more'n four foot two and had found a way to live with that—there was a woman lived on Park Avenue. She was rich, talented, beautiful; but she wasn't happy. She wanted a baby. Craved it, prayed for it, worked for it, did everything right. Never smoked, never drank. Saw the specialists; took the pills. Stuck herself with needles every day. Lay with fingers crossed and legs apart as some doc put four cells into a warm nest. (Meanwhile her husband, lucky bastard, merely had to jack off into a plastic cup and pass it to the nurse, and sign the cheques. Nice.)

She went ten rounds of hope and heartbreak, never let the pain show. She would've gone longer—husband could certainly afford it—but the docs finally broke it to her that if none of them stuck after ten, it probably ain't never gonna happen. She won't give up; keeps hoping; keeps praying. Then out of the blue—a miracle.

Comes a cold December day, her baby's born. The price? Unfortunately, her death. Well, it happens.

Beautiful baby, they say. I've seen the grown-up result; *beautiful*'s the word, damn straight. Blue eyes, black hair, porcelain skin, rosy mouth. Doting father did what parents of his class do—freakin' baffles me, this—and sent him to a boarding school just as soon as he was old enough.

Then got married again, just for good measure.

Wife Number Two had even worse luck conceiving than Jakey's mom. Makes you wonder who the weak link was really, don't it? Naturally, she took against Jakey, the living reminder of Number One. Meanwhile, Jakey's growing up . . .

What—you wanna hear about *me* now? Yeah, that's

why you'll never win the Pulitzer, pal. Always getting distracted by the minor characters.

Okay, I'll bite.

I grew up—

Ha. There's the first one. If you want to survive this cold, bad world as a dwarf, you gotta grow a thick skin *real* fast. Oh, and pick what you're gonna call yourself. That's fundamental.

Terminology's tricky. *Midget* offends just about everybody, but how about the alternatives? *Dwarf* is strange, exotic, faerie, Hobbity; like we're a separate species; make of that what you will. *Little person* is inclusive, but maybe *dismissive*, you know? *Nothing but low and little* . . . hey, you know how it is; hang around the theatre long enough, you absorb that stuff by osmosis. *Person with dwarfism*—ah, don't even get me started.

Well, okay; you asked. *Person with dwarfism* works if you're something else even more extraordinary. A surgeon (there are some) can pull off *Person with dwarfism*. But trust me, you really gotta go some before *dwarf* is only the second most interesting thing about you. Me? I'm of average intellect, average tastes, averagely dextrous, born into an average Brooklyn family (dad's a plumber, mother's a nurse). God gave me just one extraordinary difference—one thing that makes me stand out (ha!) in a crowd. Me, I'm a Dwarf.

And that's all you're getting, pal. This is Jakey's story, remember?

So, Jakey's childhood. He don't talk about it much—sweet kid, never complains—but I can see the signs. Been there myself. Ain't nothing like a highly visible disability to make those teenage years stick in the memory. My defence was a mean right hook—one advantage, you're the right height to hit 'em where it hurts.

But, still and all, I didn't have it as tough as Jakey did.

There's this *belief* about all-male boarding schools, you see. Which ain't too wide of the mark, apparently—but not how you'd think. Some of it's about who's top dog. More of it's about grossing each other out. Mostly it's a substitute, an outlet; let's face it, ain't much hornier than a fifteen-year-old schoolboy. Critical point—none of it's considered gay.

What does make you gay, though, is falling in love.

Which is kinda where we came in, ain't it?

Gotta be honest, that ain't my scene. I love Jakey to bits, but I never looked at him from under my eyelashes and thought, *hmmm*. But hey, dull world if we all want the same thing, right? Jakey always knew who he was. Knew to keep quiet, too. Boys spot *that* one, they'll kick you out and hunt you down, no mercy.

I swear, I sometimes think boys are fucking feral animals until the age of twenty. People say girls are worse. Ain't never found that myself. Girls, in my experience, are *nice*. Comforting. Supportive. Concerned. Warm. Soft. Welcoming. *Loving*. Boys, on the other hand . . . .

So. Jacob White, eighteen, Park Avenue, poor little rich boy in his final year. Paul Hunter, twenty-five, making a poor boy's journey through Med School and teaching Latin to pay the bills until his residency comes through. Paul took prep—that's home-room for WASPs—two weeks before end of term. Jakey saw blond hair, tanned skin, footballer's build. Paul saw Jakey drop his books.

'Watch it, Snowy,' he said, and passed them back. Electricity when their hands touched; that sudden, certain knowledge. Minutes, stretching into days, carefully not making eye contact. That feeling, making both their hearts pound. Scary as hell when it hits you like that; someone you couldn't, shouldn't, *mustn't* . . . but God knows you just can't beat it.

Both of them counting the days till the end of term. A note left in a pigeon hole.

Have I ever been in love, what the — ?

Ah, forget about it, I'm just yankin' your chain. You really wanna know, I'll tell you. I'll be totally honest: ain't never had time for it. That's not *I don't see the point*, by the way, that's literally *haven't had the time for it*. A career in entertainment don't make for stable personal relationships. Still, one day, if I meet a girl who likes me for *me*, not just my body . . .

Yeah, I know. You wanna hear about my job, don't you? Maybe later. This is a love story I'm telling you, and a story about shitty parenting. Back to Jakey.

So, was it love, that day on Park Avenue? Who knows? I always reckon you can't put too much faith in the lure of the forbidden, and That Feeling. Still, the way Jakey described it . . .

Wicked Stepmother was out, buying shoes, getting Botox, *something*, I don't know. Dad never got in before nine at night. Whole palace, just for them. After the obligatory awkward tour — Paul baffled by its sheer size, Jakey massively embarrassed, like *Yeah, I know, sorry, my dad's really* really *rich . . .* — they somehow got past it and into each other's arms.

Fit together like lock and key, apparently. Oh, what — too graphic? Okay. Try *hand and glove*. Still too *penetrative*? Ah, you're obsessed. How about *moon and stars*?

Yeah, too romantic. Apple pie and vanilla ice-cream? Too clean-cut. Roy Rogers and Trigger? Too horsey.

So try this. They fit together the way you *do* fit together when everything goes right; when their touch sets you on fire, when there's nothing in this world but the two of you and the occasional moan or whisper, *Like that? Just there? More? Now?* And all the time you know the answer; you're only asking because it drives you wild to hear them, knowing it's *you* making them feel that good, that needy, that desperate, my God, ain't nothing beats that feeling when it's right and sweet and perfect, vulgar and sacred all at once, and so fucking beautiful you think you're going to die—

Ahem. Sorry. Got a little distracted there.

Coulda got away with it too if they'd only stopped there, but ain't a pair of lovers anywhere knows when to put the brakes on. Paul took Jakey into his stepmother's dressing room to play.

It's freakin' *haunting* you, ain't it? Eaten up with curiosity about about how I keep the wolf from the door. All right; Dwarf Career Guidance 101.

I had nice parents, wonderful, in fact—made me welcome, loved me to bits. Supportive church. Little (!) sister who didn't take too much advantage of her big (!!!) brother. A shitty high (ho ho ho) school experience, plenty of not-very-good-natured ragging, a few beatings, until I got the hang of that right hook I mentioned. Turned eighteen; time to choose a career.

You're four foot two with an Achon Dwarf's mobility issues, there's a whole bunch of stuff you can't do. Manual work's hard, verging impossible. Forget the skilled stuff—building, plastering, plumbing, car repair—even the *unskilled* stuff is mostly outta reach (you spotting these for yourself yet?). Can't even wait tables, except as a novelty. Of course, they're supposed to adapt for workers with disabilities, but for minimum wage plus tips, you got to be realistic and ask who'll bother.

Besides, why do something dull when the Man Upstairs gave you a way out?

Jakey's kinda lean, but he ain't no Vera Wang size two, which is what Wicked Stepmother was on her wedding day. Still, they let out the laces and got him into it somehow. Then Paul got going with the cosmetics.

Sometimes, drag's grotesque, a bad parody of female-ness. Sometimes, it's beyond beautiful. Guess which Jakey was when Paul was finished.

They gazed into the mirror, young and fresh and flushed. Hands roaming, mouths warm, that soft laughter that comes easy to lovers. Then —

Oh, come on. You *know* what happened next.

Well, she walked in, and she looked at them, and she laughed. She'd waited for this day, this opportunity, her whole married life. One powerful, vengeful woman; two scared boys who were right where she wanted them. Paul and Jakey clinging to each other. Wicked Stepmother triumphant. Gay don't play well in the rarified heights of Park Avenue.

'Your father will die of shame,' she told Jakey.

'It's nothing to be ashamed of,' said Paul firmly.

'You be quiet,' she told him. 'Jacob, think of your father. You can't let him know his *only son* is a *pervert* . . .' Loving every second.

Jakey, desperate but determined: 'I can't change who I am.'

And Wicked Stepmother, like a striking snake: 'Then you'll not spend another minute under my roof.'

Paul said,

'You're just jealous because he's so much prettier than you are.'

Sometimes the truth ain't such a hot idea.

See, Wicked Stepmother's pretty, but Jakey's mother was something more. *Haunting*. She was an actress before she married Marcus. Occasionally someone runs into Jakey, and they're like, 'My *God*, you look like her . . . Anya's boy, right?'

So that did it, all right, you betcha. The truth hurts. Hurt people aren't nice.

You know, I met her once. Jakey's mama, that is.

Bet you didn't expect *that*, did you? But the stage is a cold-hearted bitch of a mistress; even the raving beauties gotta pay their dues. She started as—oh, let's say, an *exotic dancer*.

You can stop counting on your fingers, by the way—I ain't *that* old. She was gone before my time, off into the stratosphere, until Marcus White caught her in his golden net. She wasn't happy. Park Ave and Mrs White didn't quite measure up. One bright March day, she came back—see the Old Place, catch a few shows. Caught mine. Lotta gals do.

You know the old proverb, *a fool's bauble is a lady's plaything*? Course, I ain't no fool, not the way they meant it, anyway; but a lot of people wonder about Dwarfs that same way. Made a living off that my whole adult life. Made a lot of love off it, too.

But just for once, I didn't feel like that was it. It was more like—she was trying to reconnect with something.

Her old life, maybe. Who she used to be. Whatever it was, I wasn't complaining.

Most beautiful thing I ever saw.

Christ, where was I?

Back on Park, Paul laughed.

'It's okay,' he said to Jakey. 'You're coming home with me.'

'I'll get you fired,' she told Paul.

They stared at her.

'Fired and out of Med School,' she continued. 'Fucking schoolboys won't impress the Professional Ethics board. You're never going near him again. Try, and I'll find out. I'll find out, and I'll *end* you.'

Long silence. Everyone stares at everyone else. All three knew she meant it. All three knew she could.

And here's where my story and Jakey's collide.

Only one place Paul knew to bring him. I open the door and there's the young man I tipped off about the gig at St Ethelred's, desperate, panicked. In his wake, a boy with the face of a long-dead woman I'd never forgotten.

'Hey,' I said, looking up at them. They looked awkward, giant. The apartment's built for me, you see, for *us*. The seven of us that make up Small and Mighty. Put a non-Dwarf in here, suddenly *they're* the freak. Naturally, that satisfies. But Paul's a friend.

'Rough night?' I asked.

Paul nodded.

'Come on in.'

So, yeah. Paul and I worked the same turf for a while; all kinds of paths cross in the fleshpots of Forty-Second and

Broadway. Not precisely the same, mind you. He's your classic one-season wonder, pretty and forgettable. Me and my six *compadres*, we've got stamina. Girls'll still be paying to see us strip to the bone long after Paul's looking at his bald-spot and his beer-gut and wondering where it all went wrong.

You want to say *exploitation*, don't you? Ah, that's okay. Plenty out there in the little-people community think I'm a fuckin' traitor to the cause, making it harder for everyone else like us.

But here's the way I see it. Sometimes, God makes someone totally ordinary and gives them just one extraordinary gift. Anyone say to Elvis, *Forget that voice and that ear, stay in Memphis and rot*? God takes the daughter of a waitress and a hospital porter, gives her a pretty face and a blinding figure — who says to her, *Fuck Hollywood, stack shelves instead*?

Say he made you five eleven with a skinny frame, great cheekbones and no bad angles. You gonna turn down five years on the catwalks? Remember — ain't nothing special about you but the one glorious fact that you're beautiful.

Skin work? Okay, now we're getting into exploitation, sure. But again — *only one thing makes you special*. Glorious tits. Fantastic pecs and a huge cock. A body people pay to stare at. You'd say no? Really? You reckon? Yah, that's because you've never been poor and average.

Last question. Say God gave you a *different* kind of body people would pay to see. Say everywhere you go, people stare. Can't help themselves. They see you, they stop, they stare. Undress you with their eyes. Wonder what you're like underneath. Every hour, eyes moving over you. Never stops. Not for one minute.

Now who the hell wants to say I can't take my clothes off and get paid for it?

'Rafael,' I said, stuck up an arm in Jakey's general direction. He took it gravely, no embarrassment about stooping. His hand was like ice. 'You look like your mom.'

'Did you know my mom?' asked Jakey, baffled.

'Rafael knows everyone,' said Paul.

'I do,' I said, deadpan. 'He need a place to stay?'

'Is that okay?' asked Paul.

'You don't mind a Dwarf-sized bed, sure. You'll come in handy getting stuff off high shelves.' That's like a common-sense acid test, by the way; clearly in a custom-built apartment, we don't have too many places we can't reach with a stool.

Mark and Joe drifted in.

'One of Rafael's strays,' said Mark with a grin. 'What's your name?'

'Jakey,' said the boy with Anya's face.

'Mark.'

'Joe.'

Everyone shook.

'There's four more,' I said. 'Finlay, Jack, Andreas, Leroy. We're a stage act. Strippers. Just so's you know.'

Jakey took this calmly, the way you take everything calmly when your world's blown apart. He was swaying on his feet.

Paul turned to Jakey.

'I'm so sorry, Snowy . . . I—I—'

About to say the words that can either melt your heart, or tear it right out of your chest.

'Don't,' I said.

Paul looked baffled.

'Leave the kid his heart at least,' I said, and held the door open.

They looked at each other. Felt the charge between them right across the room.

Paul left before the tears spilled. I showed Jakey to bed. He was out like a light in ten seconds flat.

'Don't,' I said, over coffee this time.

'I have to see her,' said Jakey.

'Won't no good come of it,' I warned. 'The woman's poison.'

'I have to try.' Big blue eyes looking at me over the top of the mug. We have just one chair in the place for non-Dwarves; I was on the top step of the kitchen stool. We were at equal height; quite a novelty.

'Listen to Rafael,' said Finlay, wandering in and dropping a plate in the sink. 'He knows what he's talking about.'

Jakey's too nice to argue. Could see he was going anyway.

'Don't say I didn't warn you,' I told him. 'That one, she'd eat your heart if she could, and relish every bite. Meet her somewhere public.'

Finlay laughed out loud.

'You think she'll get *violent*?'

'Just you make sure,' I said. 'Coffee at Sak's. She'll like that. Chance to waste some money while she's there.'

I followed him, although blending in ain't my strong suit. Wicked Stepmother was blonde, skinny, beautiful—a bombshell in her day, still looked good. *Still*—the word women dread, the word that means *for now, but for how much longer?* Still groomed and toned enough to pull off an azure bodycon dress and skyscraper heels at one in the afternoon.

Took his hands; looked loving from a distance. Body

language easy to read. *I over-reacted, Jacob. We'd love to welcome you back, if . . .* Jakey's face wary but hopeful. Then the killer; *I have these brochures . . .* papers passed across the table, Wicked Stepmother talking faster now, blood-red fingernails stabbing. Jakey shaking his head: *no.* Narrowed eyes and whispered words. She stood up, towering over him, six foot and change on those heels, enough to scare the shit out of Attila the Hun. People turned to look. Notes thrown on the table and she was outta there, carrier bags dripping off her arm. Jakey tried to stand, couldn't make it. Everyone staring, nobody helping. Could see the cogs turning: *was he her bit on the side? Was she paying him off? I wonder how much . . . ?*

I scrounged a paper bag from a counter, ambled over to Jakey. Rubberneck factor goes up several thousand per cent — *Man, now there's a* — look, hon, it's a — *whaddya call them these days, anyway?* I waved and smiled amiably, which put them right off further staring. Useful trick.

Jakey's having a full-on panic attack; turning blue around the lips, trying to breathe and failing. I give him the paper bag to breathe into, and gradually he calms down. People peek; I stare back. They look away first.

Leaflets for sexual reorientation programmes. *Think yourself straight.* Yeah, seriously.

'She told you if you didn't enrol, your father would never see you again,' I said.

'How — did you —'

'Just concentrate on breathing. How do I know? Told you, Jakey, the woman's poison. Cut her off.'

'She's between me and my dad,' he whispered. 'I have to keep trying.'

'Like hell.'

Knew he wouldn't listen. Poor kid.

'Thank you,' said Jakey, that night in the kitchen. 'I don't know how to—you're like a guardian angel.'

I waggled my eyebrows at him.

'You know I'm straight, right?' Jakey threw a tea-towel. 'Just warning you—don't go getting any ideas.'

'Why *are* you single?' he asked.

'Never found time to fall in love.'

'But you're *always*—'

'Oh, you bet.'

'And you never loved any of them?'

'Perk of the job. Girls are curious, see. Urban legend about people like me. Mother Nature makes up for what she withheld in height by . . . ah . . . *over-endowing* us in just one department. They want to find out. More'n happy to oblige.'

'Don't you mind?'

'*Mind*?' I laughed. 'Jakey, I'm not that complicated. I get plenty of easy, joyful sex with pretty women. What's to mind?'

He looked at me, those big blue eyes looking right into my soul. Weird to be on the receiving end.

'Argh, don't *do* that. You're *right*, okay? It gets old. There, you made me say it. Happy now?' Jakey grinned. 'Don't look so smug. I think you'll find you got the same problem . . . .what? We're both freaks. You're freakishly beautiful, and me . . .' I shrugged. 'So it goes. Pass the coffee.'

We sat in silence for a while.

'So is it true?' he asked suddenly.

'Is what true?'

'What the girls all—'

I looked at him in disbelief.

'Did you just ask to see my *cock*?' Jakey blushed crimson. I laughed. 'Get outta here.'

❦

Time passes. Jakey's sweet, a pleasure to have about the place, but I can tell he ain't really healing. A few weeks later and I just—get that feeling. He's got this look, and I know, I freakin' *know*, he's called her again, begged for a meeting. And she agreed, sweet as honey, because why not? What's she got to lose?

Twenty-four hours later, I'm tailing him to a chic little restaurant in downtown Manhattan. She's waiting, scarlet nails tapping, wearing sunglasses inside, like a film star, which is exactly what she looks like. I take a table behind a pot plant, order a coffee, watch how it plays.

This time it's a different approach. Body language more urgent, less loving. *This is killing your father,* she's telling him. And Jakey trying to stand up to her: *I want to make him happy, but I can't change who I—*

Wicked Stepmother isn't having it. She's jabbing at the air again, jab jab jab jab jab, those nails like weapons. Jakey flinches, and who can blame him? *Choose this life and you're dead to both of us. He wants you to be a man, Jacob, to follow him into the business.* Jakey fighting back: *If he wants me to join the company I will, but who I fall in love with is—* Wicked Stepmother forces a few tears. If it wasn't for Jakey, I'd laugh. But he's got twenty years less experience than me; all he sees is the woman his father loves, crying.

She takes out a compact, dabs at her nose. Then a heavy, metal comb, tidying a stray strand.

You have to try, she tells him. *How you could do this to the memory of your mother—*

And finally she's gone too far, even for Jakey; he gets his rag out at last. A universal lull in the conversation, and I don't have to fill in the blanks, because we all hear him say it: 'My mother wouldn't have cared that I'm gay.'

Everyone stares, and not in the way she likes. She's furious, humiliated, caught out. She's holding that comb. I see it coming, but I can't stop it. One flick of the wrist and it's buried in Jakey's scalp, blood everywhere, and she's storming out of the restaurant.

A trip to the ER, then back to the kitchen, scene of all life's deepest conversations. I was getting ready for work, stitching on fresh sequins. Jakey took over the sewing so I could iron a shirt.

'Why do you do it, Rafael?' he asked.

I laughed.

'Tell him why we do it, Joe,' I called over my shoulder.

Joe ambled in, sombrero perched on the back of his head.

'Because it's *fun*,' he said, big shit-eating grin, and ambled out again.

Jakey looked at me and shook his head.

'Oh, what? You think it ain't a scream up on that stage, hearing them gasp and cheer?'

Jakey kept looking at me. I gestured around the apartment.

'Look around,' I said. 'We tour Vegas every summer. Christ, that place is a gold mine — we could make it on what we get just in those six weeks if we had to, the rest of the year's gravy. We're high demand, a novelty act that never gets old — I've been doing this nearly twenty years, they still scream to see us go all the way down.'

'Don't you mind?' he said, still sewing on sequins.

'Mind what?'

'Being treated like a freak?'

So I gave him the whole spiel, the one I give everybody. You work with what the Man Upstairs gives you; I got just this one thing; people stare anyway; blah, blah,

blah, blah, blah. Bada-bing. Ten thousand times I musta made that speech; never had anyone argue, even when they still felt it was wrong. Jakey's the one in ten thousand who had an answer.

'Why do you think being a dwarf is the only thing that makes you special?' he asked.

Well, that shut me up. I stared. Nearly burnt the shirt. Took the iron off just in time.

'You're amazing,' he said. 'You help *everyone*. You *fix* people. You took me in. You got Joe on the wagon and his life back on track—'

'Joe was just ready to stop drinking,' I interrupted. 'Nothing to do with me.'

'—and you convinced Finlay life was worth living. Don't look at me like that, Rafael, *please*—Andreas told me about the overdose.'

'All I did was—'

'And that girl, what was her name, Ellie, Molly, you know who I mean—'

'—'

'You got her into treatment. Now she's at college. How tall you are—that's *nothing*, compared to what you do for people in trouble. You're a life-saver.'

'So let me save *you*,' I said, stung. 'Don't let that bitter, spiteful, prejudiced *witch* screw you over. Drop her, Jakey. Drop her and live your life and move on.'

'I *can't*,' said Jakey, despairing. 'I can't—they're all I've got—'

We looked at each other in silence. Then Jakey handed over the sequinned pants.

'You could be more than this,' he said sadly.

'*So could you*,' I said.

Another long silence.

'Couple of screw-ups,' I said cheerfully, and got dressed.

Time passes; I can see Jakey ain't getting better. He's lost his home, his parents, his school friends, his lover and his future, and he's living with seven exotic performers and helping out around the house in exchange for board and lodging. Enough to blow anyone's circuits, no? He's stuck, he can't move on, and try as I might, I can't get him past it. He was set on seeing her again, to try the impossible, convince her to talk to his father, beg her if necessary, promise anything she wanted—anything except the one thing she'd asked him for, to change his essential nature. I knew it was coming, couldn't stop it. Wanted to. *Couldn't.* Told him not to. Told him to leave it. Yelled a bit. Quite a lot, actually. Had a bad feeling, like the time Joe relapsed; you see it coming, you're still powerless. Life in slow motion.

Followed him again, one last time. By now I don't think she even cares about the outcome. She's just loving that she's got power over this boy who looks like her dead rival, who'll never get old because she died before it could happen. While Wicked Stepmother gets older every day, seeing the truth in the mirror, and who *knows* what Marcus is up to on those little jaunts to Europe? All she's got left is power; power, and the thrill of using it.

I watched as they rehashed the same tired old ground. She had her claws in him good; knew just where to hurt him and how. Burned me up to see the pain on his face, the pleasure on hers.

And then—

Ah, still makes me sick to think about it. Gimme a minute, would you . . . ?

Okay. So. They were outside by this time, the anger

too big for the restaurant. Right by them's a street vendor selling fruit—pears, peaches, strawberries, apples. God, the apples.

Still don't know if she meant it.

Jakey turned away, started to cross the street.

She called his name. Tossed him an apple. Peace offering? Parting gesture? Who knows? He stopped on a reflex, caught it.

Taxi tried to swerve. Couldn't. Mowed him down.

Still don't know if she meant it.

Off the street and straight into a nightmare. Jakey in the ICU, hooked up to wires, machines, drips. Joe said the oxygen tent reminded him of a Perspex coffin. I told him what I thought about that and he never said it again, but the image was planted. The doctors reckoned he was in there somewhere, but Jakey wasn't giving any sign.

Some or other of us visited every day, all seven of us sometimes; made the nurses' day every time. Jakey never moved, never spoke. Shaved head, bruises, still beautiful.

Wicked Stepmother never showed.

You're wondering where his father was, aren't you?

See, here's the thing. Ain't nobody on this earth who's one hundred per cent anything. We're all a mass of contradictions. *I contain multitudes*, as they say. Off-stage comedians are shy. Grey-suit accountants dig bunkers and hoard bottled water and beans. And captains of industry—so I've been told by women who, forgive me, are in a position to *know*—are very often pussy-whipped.

Makes a weird sense, I guess. You spend all day being a ball-breaking SOB, when you go home, you've had enough.

Consequence of that; division of power. You rule the world. She rules the roost.

Plus, there's the fact that *Jakey looked just like her*, like Anya. Anya died for Jakey. Her life for his; any mother would make that trade in a heartbeat. But from Marcus White's perspective—the love of his life for an aching heart, an empty bed, and a baby he was only luke-warm for in the first place? You'll remember he sent Jakey to boarding school as soon as he could.

Does that explain it?

No, you're right. Nothing does; nothing in this world. His son—his blood and bone—lying in that hospital bed. Still, he didn't show.

Knowing that, I understood at last what sent Anya—Mrs White by then—to a strip club she used to work in, and then a stranger's arms in the dressing room afterwards, all those years ago.

Weeks pass. Violet called from the hostel; kid on the run, hostel full, any chance . . . ? I knew the second I met him I couldn't help much; some damage goes too deep. He stayed three nights, then left. Hurt like hell; was I losing my touch? Couldn't save Jakey either.

Still went to the hospital, every day, clockwork. Don't really pray as a rule, but I prayed then. Wanted so much to fix him, never wanted anything so much in my life. Jakey and Anya; that same unforgettable face, beautiful to the bone. Nothing I could do.

'Christ, Jakey,' I said one afternoon, perched uncomfortably on the visitor's chair. 'What's it gonna take to get you out of this?'

Nothing, of course. Just machine noises, the hiss of the ventilator.

'I wanted to help you,' I told him. 'I wanted to *help* you!'

Silence.

'What do you *want* from me?' I yelled. 'What do I have to do? Come on, Jakey, help me out here! Gimme a God-damn sign!'

Silence.

I slid off the chair, went to the door. Reached for the door handle. Couldn't quite get the bastard. *Hate* it when that happens. I kicked the door in frustration, got it open, went outside. Kicked the wall for good measure, then a trolley. A bunch of papers fall off a notice board, a bunch of folders fall off the trolley.

And then I'm staring at three pieces of paper at my feet.

First, a vile motivational poster: kitten asleep in a wastepaper basket with a picture of a tiger, and the caption *When you dream, dream BIG.*

Second, a brochure on hospital psychiatric services. Last little paragraph on the back's entitled *Ever Thought About Becoming A Counsellor?*

Third, some sucker's medical notes. No-one I knew, nothing I understood; all that mattered was the signature. *Dr Paul Hunter.*

Look me in the eye and tell me that wasn't a sign.

I called home, told Leroy Small and Mighty would be down one man that night. Then I started combing the hospital for Paul. Took me hours; I couldn't remember what he'd specialised in. Turned out to be Emergency. He looked shattered, so I forgave him for nearly falling over me.

'What the —' He looked down, exasperated, then amazed. 'Rafael!'

I took him to ICU, seven floors up, filled him in on

the way. By the time the lift gets there, he's pacing the floor. Outside Jakey's door, I stopped him.

'You better be sure,' I said. 'Jakey's been through *enough*. You man enough for this, Paul? You gonna run out on him again?'

'I was scared, I—'

'If nothing's changed, don't go in. Leave him in peace.'

'She could have ended my career.'

'Then walk away.'

'*No.*'

'Why not?'

'Because I love him.'

'*Love?*' I laughed. 'You were together for what, six hours?'

'Sometimes that's all you need.'

'You walked out on him once,' I reminded him. 'Left him with me instead.'

'Please.'

I glared at him.

'You give me your word?'

He nodded. I stepped aside. Paul stumbled to his knees by the bed. I heard him sob, and kiss Jakey on the mouth.

You tune the monitors out, after a while. Only notice when the sound changes. Suddenly I'm hearing machine noises again, and it's better than Elvis, better than Waits, better than Bach, better than your mother singing you to sleep on a cold night, and I turn and leave the room, my heart too big for my chest, filling all the emptiness inside me and forcing tears out over my cheeks, because Jakey's woken up at last, and I've done my job, and my part in their love story's over.

One last thing. I wanted to fix Jakey, the way I always want to. He was the first one wanted to fix me in return.

Small and Mighty still tours every summer in Vegas, but I'm not with them any more. I rang that number on the back of the brochure, signed up for the course. Now I'm fixing people on a full-time basis, getting paid and everything. I'm a *counsellor with dwarfism*. On an exceptional day, I'm just *a counsellor*.

Oh, and a husband. I met Rosalie the first day of the training. We hit it off just right. After years of casual sex, I wasn't sure I had the stamina for more than a week, plus I wanted to be sure she wasn't just one more girl with a dwarf-curious itch to scratch, so we took our time. Worth the wait. Jakey and Paul were witnesses at the wedding.

For the record, she's five eight, and beautiful. Talk about Beauty and the Beast . . .

. . . but, of course, that's a whole other fairy tale.

Acknowledgements

I would like to thank the editors of Legend Press where 'Interview #17' previously appeared in the short story anthology *Ten Journeys*, May 2010.

I'd also like to say a huge thank you to the following people:

Thank you to Jen Hamilton-Emery at Salt, for taking a chance on a new writer and publishing *New World Fairy Tales*.

Thank you to my lovely American friends for teaching me to talk properly, and for patiently answering my endless questions about turnpikes, stoops, sweaters, stoves, rugs and frantic 3 a.m. emails along the lines of 'So, could you talk to me about High School?' or 'What's a really boring handgun?'. You've been the best writer's group anyone could ask for and your turn is surely coming soon.

Thank you to my friends and family, who have all been patiently telling me for years, 'You know, you should really try and be a writer. No, really, you should' and never once getting irritated with me when I completely failed to pay attention. Sorry it took me so long to start listening. A special thank you to Rebecca and Ben, for never once doubting—not even for a moment.

Thank you most of all to my husband Tony. As for all the other important times, you've been my rock and this would never have happened without you.

Finally, I'd like to acknowledge the debt I owe to Jacob and Wilhelm Grimm, on whose mighty shoulders I have had the temerity to stand.